How many times had she fantasised about kissing that mouth? Too many to count.

And there it was, right in front of her.

Her pulse kicked up another notch as the devil whispered, *Kiss him,* and she contemplated doing just that.

That would *definitely* wake him up.

But what if he rejected her advances? It would be embarrassing and awkward. For a *very* long time. It would probably even kill her. She'd probably die of mortification on the spot.

It would certainly be hard to come back from.

Another sinful whisper. *But what if he doesn't?*

In a few short months Luke would be heading back to London, and the thought that she might never get another opportunity to show him how she felt suddenly scared her a hell of a lot more.

Screw it.

And the devil smiled.

Dear Reader

When my editor approached me with the idea of doing a duet with Ally Blake last February my first reaction was, *Hell, yeah!* I adore Ally's writing, and she's just all-round fun to work with! Throw in some glorious Australian sunshine, a tropical resort and some bikinis and how could I resist? But let me tell you Ally got the raw end of the deal. I had a hectic schedule last year, and while she was planning her book for the duet—which is, OMG, knock-you-out-of-the-park fabulous!—I still had another three books to finish...

But her enthusiasm for the project and her love affair with Pinterest kept drawing me into the world of the Tropicana. When I'd finally cleared my decks I was all fired up to start.

I absolutely adored creating the world of the Tropicana Nights—an old-fashioned resort from yesteryear, when families holidayed together and entertainment was simple—with Ally. Creating Luke and Claudia was fabulous also. Two people who grew up together with the Tropicana as their playground, who both love the resort in their own ways but who clash over their polar opposite visions for its future.

I love the title of this book. THE HEAT OF THE NIGHT is very apt because—trust me—things soon get pretty fired up between these two childhood friends. They might not be able to agree on what's good for the Tropicana, but their bodies are perilously in sync.

Ahh...those summer nights...

I hope you enjoy their tumultuous tumble into love. And if you haven't read Ally Blake's HER HOTTEST SUMMER YET then run out and get it! You won't be sorry!

Love

Amy

Those Summer Nights
In Crescent Cove find sun, sea and steamy nights...

Read the first book in this sultry duet:
HER HOTTEST SUMMER YET
by Ally Blake!

THE HEAT OF
THE NIGHT

BY
AMY ANDREWS

MILLS
BOON®

MORAY COUNCIL LIBRARIES & INFO.SERVICES	
20 37 40 75	
Askews & Holts	
RF RF	

First pul
by Mills
Eton Ho

Amy Andrews has always loved writing, and still can't quite believe that she gets to do it for a living. Creating wonderful heroines and gorgeous heroes and telling their stories is an amazing way to pass the day. Sometimes they don't always act as she'd like them to—but then neither do her kids, so she's kind of used to it. Amy lives in the very beautiful Samford Valley, with her husband and aforementioned children, along with six brown chooks and two black dogs.

She loves to hear from her readers. Drop her a line at www.amyandrews.com.au

Other Modern Tempted™ titles by Amy Andrews:

THE MOST EXPENSIVE NIGHT OF HER LIFE
GIRL LEAST LIKELY TO MARRY

To Ally Blake for her indefatigable enthusiasm and getting this duet off to an incredible start with two wonderful characters in Jonah and Avery.

And for getting me hooked on Pinterest.

CHAPTER ONE

LUKE HARGREAVES HAD never seen such an unholy mess in all his life. Uprooted trees competed for space amidst the smashed and splintered building debris. Dangerous electrical and glass hazards lay strewn everywhere. Only one out of the dozen buildings that made up the five-acre property where the Tropicana Nights had sprawled for forty years had survived intact.

Holy crap. The resort was never going to recover from this.

It was hard to believe standing underneath the perfect untainted blue of a tropical north Queensland sky, listening to the gentle kiss of waves as they lapped at the crescent beach fringing this idyllic tourist spot, that weather could be responsible for such violence.

That the light breeze could build to cyclonic, that the cloudless sky could blacken with ominous intent and the calm ocean could rage and pound.

Sure, cyclones were one of the hazards of living on the northern Australian coastline and the resort had sustained damage in the past from such events that regularly stalked the coast from November to March.

But never like this.

This one had been a monster and Crescent Cove's number had been up.

A decade in the UK had anaesthetised him to the dangers of tropical storms, but, looking at the destruction now, it was a miracle no one had been killed.

All thanks to Claudia.

Luke's gaze trekked from the devastated resort to the devastated figure standing on the beach, her back to the ocean as she surveyed the damage. Avery had told him Claudia was taking it all in her stride. But he knew Claudia Davis well. Too well. And her look of hopeless despair was evident even from this distance.

Somehow inside his head, despite the march of time, she'd always been a skinny six-year-old with blonde pigtails and skinned knees. And there was something just as gut-wrenchingly innocent about her today. Her ponytail fluttering in the gentle breeze, her petite frame encased in the God-awful polyester Tropicana uniform that hadn't changed since the seventies, that damn stupid clipboard she always carried around clutched to her chest.

The intense little wrinkle of her brow as if she was trying to wish it all better from the power of her mind alone.

He sighed. He was *not* looking forward to this.

He shucked off his shoes and stripped off his socks leaving them at the row of lopsided palm trees that formed a natural demarcation between beach and land. Or what was left of them anyway.

Crescent Cove's beloved palm-tree avenue, which hugged the long curve of beach, was looking equally devastated. Whole trees had been ripped out by the roots, plucked clean from the ground and thrown around as if they'd been mere matchsticks, some still lying on the path or beach wherever they'd been hurled.

It would take a lot of years to build it back to its former glory.

The hot sun beat down on Luke's neck, a far cry from chilly London, and he shrugged out of his jacket too. He undid his cuffs and rolled up his sleeves on his business shirt. He turned his phone to silent and slipped it in his back pocket. He didn't want to be disturbed when he spoke to her and he'd already had three urgent texts from the office.

Taking a deep, fortifying breath, he stepped onto the

beach and headed towards the woman he'd known nearly all his life, his footsteps squeaking in the powdery sand.

Claudia stared at the wreck before her, a sense of helplessness and despair overwhelming her. She should have known that only a cyclone named Luke could cause this much damage.

She refused to give into the harsh burn of tears scalding her eye sockets.

She would not cry.

Crying was for wimps and she was *not* a wimp. She'd spent a year of her life renovating her beloved family resort and just because it lay in a shambled ruin in front of her didn't mean it was time to give into a fit of girly histrionics.

She held tight to the comfort of her clipboard. They *would* recover from this. They *had* to.

But how? a little voice asked somewhere in the back of her brain, bleating away in time to the distant drone of generators that had filled the air for days now. The same voice she'd been hearing every time she stood on the beach and was confronted by the true horror of the destruction of the only home she'd ever known.

Well, there was the main resort building—the original structure—for a start. Even now its white stucco façade gleamed beneath the full morning sun like a beacon amidst the rubble, its sturdy stone construction having somehow miraculously survived Mother Nature's fury with only minimal damage.

How, Claudia had no idea.

How had the dinosaur—or White Elephant as Luke had coined it—managed to survive when the newer edition bungalows, made to the highest ever cyclone specifications, had perished?

It didn't make any sense. It had been four days since Cyclone Luke, a huge category-five juggernaut, had crossed the coast right on top of them, and it still didn't make any sense.

None of it did.

Tears threatened again and Claudia blinked them back. She refused to cry as Avery had done. Tears wouldn't get the Tropicana back on its feet and Claudia was determined to hold it all together if it killed her. She'd been doing that since Luke had deserted her to run the place by herself, since their respective parents had handed the keys over to them and entrusted twenty years of their life's work to their children.

She would not be cowed by the mammoth task ahead of her just as she'd refused to be cowed by Luke's ultimatum this time last year to have the resort turned around in twelve months—or else!

She hadn't needed him to elaborate on his threat—and it really hadn't been an issue because she *had* turned it around. They'd had a bumper summer, there was money in the bank and they'd been poised to welcome their best ever winter season in over a decade.

And then along came Cyclone Luke. As determined as the other Luke in her life to take away everything she'd ever known and loved.

'Bloody hell, Claude. You're never going to recover from this.'

Claudia blinked as the eerily familiar voice behind her caused everything inside her—her heartbeat, her breath, the metabolism in her cells—to come to a standstill.

Luke?

She turned and there he was. Standing right there. Every tall, lean, clean-shaven inch of him. Close enough to touch. Close enough to feel a very familiar pull down deep and low.

Luke.

The boy she'd hero-worshipped, the teenager she'd crushed on, the man who'd disappointed her more than she'd ever thought possible when he'd turned his back on their legacy.

You're never going to recover from this?

His words were like a jolt to the chest from a defibrillator and then everything surged back to life. Her lungs dragged in a swift harsh breath, her heart kicked her in the ribcage with all the power of a mule, her cells started metabolising again at warp speed.

You're never going to recover from this?

Oh, no! He had to be kidding. This *had* to be a monumental joke. *A very bad one.*

But no, here he was, in a freaking business shirt and trousers. O*n the beach.* Gloating. A tsunami of emotion Claudia had been stuffing down for four days—hell, for the last year—rose in her chest and demanded to be expressed.

'What the hell are you doing here?'

Luke's eyes widened at the distinct lack of welcome turning her normally chirpy voice deeper. Darker. He shrugged. 'I saw it on the tele…I just…came.'

And he had. As much as he'd resented the weird pull this place still had over him, he couldn't *not* put in an appearance. Escaping to the other side of the world a decade ago, immersing himself in a completely different life had dulled the pull, but one look at the devastation and it had roared back to life.

Claudia blinked at his explanation, then let loose a laugh that bordered on hysteria. But if she didn't laugh she was going to cry. And it wasn't going to be dainty little London tears he was no doubt used to from his bevy of gorgeous sophisticated Brits, it was going to be a cyclonic, north Queensland snot fest.

And she'd be damned if she'd break down in front of *Luke*.

'How'd you even get here?' she demanded. 'The road is still cut in both directions.'

'Jonah picked me up in his chopper from Cairns airport.'

Claudia vaguely remembered hearing the chopper a little while ago and she silently cursed Jonah for being so damned handy. She made a mental note to tell Avery to withhold sex from him as his punishment for fraternising with the enemy.

Because as far as she was concerned, Luke Hargreaves was public enemy number one.

Not that Avery would—those two were still so loved up it was sickening.

'Well, you came, you saw,' she snapped. 'Now you can leave. Everything's fine and dandy here.'

Fine and dandy? Luke looked at the unholy wreck in front of him. It was the complete antithesis of fine and dandy. He shoved his hands in his pockets. 'I'm not going to do that, Claude.'

Claudia gave an inelegant snort. 'Why not? Isn't that what you do? Leave?'

'I thought I could...' Luke flicked his gaze to the flattened resort '...help.'

'Help?' Her voice sounded high even to her own ears. '*Now* you want to help?'

'Claude...' Luke sighed, unsurprised she was still carrying a grudge that he hadn't wanted anything to do with their parents' giant folly when they'd decided to retire and pass on the management to their children last year. 'I can help with the clean-up. And there will be partnership decisions that need to be made.'

A sudden surge of anger burned white-hot in Claudia's chest. *Partnership decisions?* What the hell? Did he think she'd be too distraught to not understand the true meaning behind such a casual announcement?

She drew herself up to her full five feet one inch, and jammed a hand on her hip. 'You think you have *the right* to waltz in here—'

Claudia broke off as a pressure—rage and something more primitive—built in her sinuses and behind her eyes. It threatened to explode and robbed her momentarily of the ability to form a coherent sentence.

'To just...*sweep* in when everything is such a bloody mess...and think you have a *right* to any decisions? You forfeited any rights when you walked away from the Tropicana last year.'

Luke tried to stay calm in the face of her anger. But Claudia always had driven him more nuts than any woman in the history of the world. She'd always been a firecracker where the resort was concerned, her petite, perennially cheerful disposition slipping quickly to growly Mummy bear when her precious Tropicana was threatened.

He kept his hands firmly buried in his pockets lest he succumb to the urge to shake her. Part of the reason she was in this mess was because she'd refused to listen to reason. If they'd gone the way he'd wanted to go with the resort they'd have been making money hand over fist as part of a bigger chain and therefore sheltered financially from such a monumental disaster.

But no. Claudia had wanted to keep the resort completely independent. Run it the way their parents had in some grand vision of yesteryear.

And he'd been too busy dealing with the disarray left by his ex, both personally and career-wise, to really care. But this mess was going to require some big decisions.

'Well, actually, that's not entirely true, is it?'

Claudia knew exactly what he was alluding to and hated that he was right. *Hated it.* But his name was still on the partnership agreement their parents had made them sign and he did have equal say—he just hadn't been interested in claiming it before today.

Claudia sighed, feeling utterly defeated all of a sudden. 'Look, I get it, you're here out of some misguided sense of responsibility. But you really don't need to worry. Everything's fine and dandy. Just go back to London. I can only deal with one Luke at a time.'

Luke was torn between picking her up and dumping her in the ocean and pulling her into his arms. 'I'm staying. I have a week off. I can help with the clean-up.'

This time Claudia's laugh did not *border* on anything—it had lapsed into full-blown hysteria.

'A week?' she demanded, her voice high and shaky. 'Well, gee, Luke, thank you for sparing *seven lousy days* out of your busy and important life to help out poor old Claude.'

She shook her head in disgust at him, the urge to slam the clipboard down on his head riding her as hard as the threatening tears. She *would not* cry!

'Take a look at this place,' she demanded, flinging her arms wide to distract from the crack in her voice. 'Do you think this is going to be cleaned up in a week?'

Luke looked. He doubted it would be cleaned up in a month. But he had a major account on the hook, one that would erase for ever the big one he'd lost because he'd foolishly trusted the woman he'd loved. He couldn't afford to spend a lot of time away. Hell, he couldn't even afford *seven lousy days.*

But he was here, wasn't he?

'Let's just take it one day at a time,' he suggested, holding onto his temper.

Claudia glared at him. 'Don't patronise me. I have an entire army of people ready, willing and able to help me clean up when we get the all-clear. We don't need someone whose heart isn't in it and who doesn't give a damn about the Tropicana.'

Luke clenched his fists in his pockets. Just because he hadn't chosen to slavishly devote himself to a forty-year-old white elephant, didn't mean he didn't care. He glared at her. 'And I suppose walking around with that damn clipboard and wearing that God-awful Hawaiian shirt and those polyester capris proves your level of give a damn?'

Claudia gasped at his insult. The uniform had been around since the beginning—it was *iconic*, damn it! But it gave her something else to focus on other than the prickle inside her nose caused by building emotion. 'I'm on duty,' she snapped.

It was Luke's turn to snort. 'For what? There's nobody here, Claude.'

Claudia held herself erect. 'I'm never off duty.'

And that, as far as Luke was concerned, was one of her problems. She was twenty-seven years old and, apart from her brief sojourns overseas with Avery every couple of years, the resort had been her entire focus.

'You really need a life,' he muttered, still smarting from her stinging judgment of him.

'*I* need a life?' She laughed again, all high and shaky. 'This from a man who wears a freaking suit to the beach.'

'I got the first flight I could,' he said. 'I went straight from work to Heathrow. I know it's hard for you to believe but there are other people in this world just as dedicated to their jobs as you are to yours. Although I think manic obsession probably fits better in your case.'

'The Tropicana isn't a *job*. It's our legacy,' Claudia snapped.

Luke shook his head as a storm of frustration and disbelief raged in his gut. God, her doggedness was infuriating.

'It's not *our legacy*. It's just an old-fashioned relic from a different time and *everybody's* moved on but you. You're not in *Dirty Dancing*, Claude, and this—' he threw his arms wide at the destruction before him '—isn't freaking Kellerman's. Johnny Castle isn't going to drop by and demand that nobody puts you in a corner.'

Claude blinked. A pain flared in the vicinity of her heart as he took everything she believed in and crushed it into the hot, white sand. Yes, she was sentimental and a romantic and she not only believed *but had proved* that there was a market for the style of resort he was so disparaging of. She just hadn't realised he'd thought so little of the things that were important to her.

It made her feel small. Insignificant. Unvalued.

And so very sad. For her and for him. His divorce sure had made him cynical.

And it was her undoing. Her vision blurred, the emotion she'd been holding back for days coming now whether she liked it or not. A solitary tear spilled down her cheek.

Luke saw the tear threaten, then fall and wished he could cut his tongue out. He'd been angry and frustrated and his words had been harsh and ill considered. Strands of her blonde hair had loosened and blew across her face, sticking to the wet tear track and her mouth.

'Claudia.' He took a step towards her.

Claudia shook her head and held up a hand to ward him off, swiping at the tear with the other, angry that he was a witness to it, that she was being weak and *sentimental* in front of him. 'Just go back to London, Luke.' She turned away, marching off, needing to get away from his toxic disregard as more tears ran down her face.

Luke watched as she turned away, marching back up the beach, her spine straight, her ponytail barely bouncing as she held her head high. He cursed his insensitivity.

That went well. *Not.*

CHAPTER TWO

Avery, Jonah, Isis and Cyrus looked up from the reception desk that had been turned into a mini war room as the glass entrance door was yanked open and a red-eyed, tear-streaked Claudia stalked inside the cavernous lobby. Jonah looked at Avery with a question in his eyes as Claudia steamed straight past them.

'Claude?' Avery called after her, her American accent echoing around the large, deserted foyer. Claudia didn't stop or reply.

'Claudia.'

This time Claudia hesitated slightly before throwing an, 'I'm fine,' over her shoulder and, 'I just need some time alone,' before hitting the wide elegant staircase that would have been perfectly at home in some maharajah's palace.

There was a worried silence as four sets of eyes watched her beat her hasty retreat to her first-floor suite.

'What was that about?' asked Cyrus, a young local guy employed at the Tropicana as a bellhop.

'I don't know,' said Isis, his sister, who usually worked Reception.

The siblings, products of hippy parents, were uncannily similar with their striking red hair and freckles.

'I think I do,' Avery said, her eyes narrowing as Luke strode up the wide front steps.

Luke, his shoes and jacket in hand, glanced at the reception desk as he entered the lobby. None of the people behind it looked very receptive.

He made his way across the expanse of mosaic tiles swirling together to form a tapestry of rich sandy tones. He diverted around colossal rugs, cushy lounge chairs and potted palms. Huge beige columns rose to the two-storey ceiling and bordered the domed mural on high. It showcased a midnight sky twinkling with stars, the edges decorated with palm leaves.

As a kid it had fascinated him endlessly; now it seemed just another relic of yesteryear.

'Luke Hargreaves,' Avery said, her voice full of accusation as he approached the desk. 'Did you make Claude cry?'

Luke glanced at Jonah, standing behind Avery, who was sending him *run away now* signals with his eyes. Jonah knew as well as Luke that Avery was Claudia's fiercest champion.

'I'm rather afraid I did.' He grimaced as he approached the desk.

Much to Luke's surprise Avery's shoulder's sagged and she said, 'Oh, thank God for that. She needed a damned good cry.'

The group all nodded in agreement, even Jonah. 'Oh, yes,' Isis agreed. 'She's been saying she's *fine and dandy* for days now.'

'Fine and dandy,' Cyrus repeated. 'Like a cracked record.'

'Well...' Luke shrugged '...mission accomplished.'

Luke was glad that little group were more relaxed and looking less like they wanted to hang, draw and quarter him. Apparently an upset Claudia was a good thing. But it didn't help his guilt...the things he'd said had been fairly unforgivable.

He felt about as low as a man could feel.

He remembered all too well how it'd felt to be idolised by her and he much preferred that feeling. Although he'd certainly developed feet of clay as far as she was concerned since declining the opportunity to give up his entire life in the UK—no matter how shambolic—and manage the resort with her.

He glanced up the stairs behind him, then back to the group. He had to go and apologise. 'Think I'll go and see how she is. Say sorry.'

Avery shook her head. 'No. That would be bad.'

Jonah agreed. 'You should give her some time to cool off, man.'

Cool off? As if anyone could cool off in this God-awful heat without the electricity that usually cooled the vast lobby into a blissful paradise. The frustration that had ridden him down at the beach returned for a second spin and a sudden rush of bone-wearying tiredness joined the mix.

He was jet-lagged to hell and sweating like a pig in his inappropriate clothes, but he had to *fix* this.

'Why didn't you tell me on the chopper ride she was this fragile?' Luke demanded of Jonah.

'She's not fragile,' Avery said, rising quickly to Claudia's defence.

'You could have fooled me,' he snorted.

'She's been working day and night organising everything like a Trojan, getting things into place so when the official all-clear comes tomorrow we can start the clean-up, not to mention having to deal with the two hundred guests we were expecting over the next few weeks.' Avery glared at him. '*And* she's been helping out in the town and at the other resorts. She's been strong, she's been a leader. She is *not* fragile.'

'Then why is she bursting into tears?'

Avery shook her head at him and Luke felt lower still.

'Because she's exhausted. Because she's stressed and worried. She's barely slept a wink in five days. Because her entire life just got blown all to hell and maybe, just maybe, she'd thought you might be the one man who really understood her devastation. None of us here can truly understand how this disaster in this place she loves so much has wounded her. Except you. Is that what you did, Luke? Did you go down to the beach and tell her you understood?'

Luke avoided the doubt and reprimand in Avery's gaze as guilt rode him again. 'I asked you how she was doing,' he said, turning to Jonah. 'You said she was fine.'

Jonah nodded. 'She is fine. *And dandy.* Considering everything she's worked for this last year has been flattened to a pulp. She's been keeping busy and putting up a good front for us all. But you're *family*, man. Your opinion has always mattered more than anyone else's.'

Luke scowled, hating that Jonah was right. He had lashed out and hurt her. 'Right,' he said after a moment. 'So I'd better go and fix it, then.'

Avery made a tutting sound and it was Luke's turn to glare. 'What?'

'I know you're a man and all and it's in your DNA to *fix* stuff but she doesn't need that. She told us she needed some time alone and a smart man would just let her do it. And probably after that she needs you to shut your mouth and just hug her.'

Jonah nodded. 'Give her some space, man. I wouldn't add insult to injury if I were you.'

Luke knew it was good advice. But he couldn't bear the fact that she was upstairs all alone crying because of the things *he'd* said. Claudia wasn't a crier—never had been. She was bouncy and cheery and peppy.

She was a ray of freaking sunshine.

And he'd made her cry. *He* was responsible for her tears.

Luke shook his head. 'Nope, sorry, can't.'

And then he was gone and four sets of eyes watched him bound up the stairs following in Claudia's footsteps.

Avery sighed. 'And I thought he was smart.'

Jonah slid a hand onto Avery's shoulder and squeezed as he pulled her gently back against his chest. 'Even smart men can be stupid where women are concerned.'

She smiled and slid her hand over the top of his. 'That's true. You were pretty dumb.'

Jonah chuckled and dropped a kiss on her temple.

'That's not going to end well, is it?' Cyrus asked his sister, agog that *anyone* would go against Claudia's express wishes.

Isis shook her head. 'His funeral.'

Luke's feet took him without conscious thought to the door of the Copacabana Suite, the room where Claudia had lived with her parents since she was six years old. He and his parents had lived next door in the Mai Tai Suite. He hesitated before he knocked—maybe she didn't reside here any more? Maybe she'd downgraded now her parents had moved on? It wasn't as if a single woman needed a massive two-bedroom suite.

But the thought was only fleeting. Claudia Davis was as sentimental as they came. No way would she have passed up the nostalgia of her childhood home. Or the view from the balcony.

He knocked. No answer.

He knocked again. Louder. Still no answer.

'Claude, I know you're in there. Open up.'

No answer.

'I can stand out here all day and knock,' he warned, even if the thought made him weary to his bones. 'Hell, I can just sit down here and wait for you to come out. You're going to have to eventually. But I'm not going back to England. I'm not going anywhere for a week so you might as well get used to it.'

Still no answer. The door remained stubbornly closed. Luke sighed and slid down the door, propping his back against the dark grain wood. He was too bloody tired to stand upright. Despite the luxury of business class he hadn't slept much on the plane—worry about the resort, *about Claudia* had unfortunately kept sleep at bay.

Luke rubbed his eyes and scrubbed at his face with his hands. He could hear the faint rasp of stubble already fighting back against the quick shave he'd managed in the restroom aboard the plane. He was used to keeping it ruthlessly smooth, and it bothered him—he really should do something about that.

After a shower. And a sleep.

In fact his whole appearance bothered him. His sleeves were rolled up haphazardly, his top three buttons were undone, his expensive business shirt felt sticky against his sweaty chest and his bare feet were still coated with traces of sand.

Luke prided himself on his appearance. He believed it had a lot to do with his success. If you looked professional clients were more likely to part with their money.

He rapped again on the door, his knuckles connecting with the wood just above his shoulder. 'Claude.'

Still no answer.

Luke looked back at his feet and rubbed his toes together to displace the sand. A fine sprinkling of gritty powder dusted the thinning, aged carpet with its palm-tree print that had graced this hallway for as long as he could remember.

As a kid roaming around the resort he'd never been without sand between his toes. He'd rarely even noticed it, for ever being chided by his mother for tracking it into the suite. He'd loved it back then.

But like everything else today, it bugged him and he leaned down with his fingers to brush it all off. His phone buzzed in his pocket and he rubbed his hands together to remove the last trace of sand before quickly answering the text.

A pair of work boots filled his vision as he hit send and he glanced up to find Jonah looking down at him dangling a key—yes, they still had real bona fide keys at the Tropicana, *of course*—from his fingers.

'This might help,' Jonah said. 'And if you tell Avery I gave it to you I will deny everything.'

Luke put the phone away and took Jonah's offering. It was the keys to the Mai Tai. He smiled. 'Thank you.'

Jonah and Luke had been friends a long time so when he reached out a hand Luke grabbed hold gratefully and let

Jonah haul him to his feet. 'Don't screw it up,' Jonah warned before retreating.

Luke made his way next door and slid the key into the lock. For twenty years the Davis family and the Hargreaves family had not only run the resort but lived right next door to each other. Somehow, *miraculously,* they'd made it through twenty years in business together and still come out as friends. Even choosing to take their trip of a lifetime together.

Luke stepped inside the suite, which looked more worn and shabby around the edges than ever. A familiar smell of old carpet, starched linen and the hibiscus air freshener that was synonymous with his childhood embraced him. He'd grown to hate that smell as his desperation to see the big wide world had grown more intense, but today it was soothing to ragged nerve endings.

He *must* be tired.

He glanced at the big king-sized bed covered in its colourful Hawaiian-style bedspread and was surprised by the overwhelming desire to leave Claudia alone as she'd requested and get some much-needed sleep. Tackle her when he could count on more than two functioning brain cells. But that solitary tear played in slow motion through his head and he placed temptation firmly behind him as he stalked to the connecting door.

A long-forgotten memory made Luke hesitate before sliding the key into the lock. When their parents had run the resort, the door was never locked. In fact it was usually left chocked open. On a hunch, he just reached for the handle.

The knob turned and the door opened.

And there, dead ahead, on a matching king-sized bed, lay Claudia, all curled up and very definitely bawling her eyes out. She was crying so hard and so loud, he didn't think she'd even heard the door swing open.

Hell, it sounded as if she were crying for Australia and going for gold.

Another spike of guilt drove a stake right between his eyes. *Crap.* He hesitated before he crossed the threshold into her room but *what the hell*? He'd come this far.

The curtains that matched the bedspread were pulled back and the balcony doors were thrown wide, admitting the magnificent tropical view. A cool ocean breeze tickled at the open neck of his shirt as he tentatively edged inside, and felt heavenly against his sweaty skin.

'Claude?'

Claudia almost leapt out of her skin as Luke's deep, rich voice reached straight into the middle of her misery and yanked her out by the roots of her hair. She sat abruptly, her tears temporarily forgotten.

'Jeez,' she said, her hand clutched to her rocketing heart, 'are you trying to scare me half to death?'

Luke stalled where he was, holding up his hands at the frightening sight of a puffy-eyed, wild-looking Claudia. Her hair was half in, half out of her ponytail, the loose bits clumped together into some kind of bird-nest-like creation, her nose and cheeks were red and she was surrounded by piles of well-used tissues.

'Sorry...I didn't mean to startle you.'

'Who gave you a damn key?' Claudia demanded, ignoring his apology. 'No, don't worry, it was Jonah, wasn't it? Bloody traitor.'

Luke took a tentative step closer. 'I just wanted to see if you were okay,' he said, avoiding selling out Jonah.

'Do I look okay?' she snapped.

Luke shook his head. She looked as if she'd been dragged through a hedge backwards. She looked angry and sad and tired.

She looked defeated.

And that probably kicked him the hardest. Claudia was a glass-half-full kind of girl.

'Oh, just go away,' Claudia groaned as the fright wore off and the surge of adrenaline mixed with her already precarious emotional state to make her feel even more edgy and vulnerable. Emotion clogged her throat and the hot scald of tears pricked at her eyes again.

She fell back against the mattress, resuming her former foetal-ball position. 'Just let me cry in peace,' she said, dragging another tissue out of the box.

Luke was torn between leaving and not having to listen to her cry and staying put, being some kind of emotional support for Claudia. Or *trying* at least.

Neither prospect thrilled him.

But the part of him that had run barefoot through the resort with her and swum with her in the ocean just across the pathway and played hide-and-seek with her amidst the resort gardens won out.

He shut his eyes, sending up a brief plea to the universe that she wouldn't jab him in the ribs or knee him somewhere a little lower as he moved around the other side of the enormous bed and climbed on.

Claudia frowned as she felt the bed give behind her. She looked over her shoulder as Luke approached on his hands and knees. 'What are you doing?' she demanded.

'I'm doing what I should, according to Avery, have done down on the beach. I'm going to hug you.'

Claudia blinked and swallowed against another threatening tide of tears. She gave an inelegant sniffle. 'If you hug me I'm just going to cry harder.'

Luke chuckled at her husky threat as he settled in behind her, slipping his arm around her waist. 'I guess that's probably kind of the point.'

Claudia's breath caught at the light tease in his voice and she looked away from him, turned to face the doorway over the other side of the room. Her back was all smooshed against his front—his big, broad, hard front—his breath was a warm caress at her neck, the slight scrape of stubble skating delicious shivers to dangerous places.

She shut her eyes, her heart racing now for an entirely

different reason. How many hot, fevered dreams had she had as a teenager about exactly this? Lying with him like this?

Minus their clothes, and her inhibitions?

Luke shut his eyes as his exhausted body revelled in being horizontal. Claudia felt stiff as a board but it was bliss to lie down and he could already feel the tug of sleep pulling at the hazy hold he had on consciousness.

How many times had they lain in her parents' bed as kids, watching reruns of Claudia's favourite television show, *The Love Boat,* while their parents finished up for the night? She'd always offered to let him watch something he wanted to but he hadn't minded—as long as whatever they were watching had ads, he was happy.

How many times had Tony, the head chef, who had been at the Tropicana for all its forty years, personally brought them up his speciality Hawaiian pizza? And how many times had he woken to his dad picking him up and carrying him to his bed next door?

But so much had happened in the intervening years to put distance between them. He'd gone away—far away. He'd rarely been back as he'd fought to establish himself in a dog-eat-dog industry. He'd got married. *And divorced.* He'd refused to come back and play when the resort was handed to him. He'd disagreed with her vision.

In short, he'd changed.

But Claudia? Claudia was still the same girl she'd always been. He'd thought less of her for that this last decade but, lying here with her now, he was immensely pleased that she was still the same old Claude.

Except she was so quiet and rigid. Taut as a bow. He wished he knew the right words to comfort her. The time when they'd been close and their conversations had been easy seemed a million years ago now.

He'd spent a decade in the cut-throat advertising game where men and women alike fought tooth and nail for an account. There wasn't a lot of softness, of emotion, in the advertising business. Nobody comforted you when you lost an account—if anything there was a certain degree of triumph at someone else's misfortune, the scent of an opportunity in the offing.

God knew he'd witnessed the pointy end of it three years ago after being the golden-haired boy for so long.

None of that helped him with right here, right now. None of that equipped him to deal with a grieving Claudia.

'Was it awful?' he whispered.

Claudia tensed as the whisper seemed to punctuate the silence like a blaring trumpet. She'd been trying not to think about that night. Trying to keep busy and organise. Trying to look ahead, not back. Not think about the howling wind and the sounds of destruction that not even a large underground cellar had insulated them from.

Her face scrunched up in a most unpleasant fashion as the fear rolled over her again and she was pleased he was behind her. A tear rolled down her cheek as she relaxed back into him.

'I was so scared,' she said, choking on a lump high and hard in her throat, trying to hold it all back but failing because Luke was here. 'I knew we were all safe down in the cellar but...it was so loud. And it destroyed everything.'

Claudia paused as the next thought formed. It was too awful to speak aloud. 'What if I can't do it?' she whispered. 'What if I fail? What if I let everybody down?'

She started to cry again and Luke finally understood the true root of her anxiety. Claudia had spent her whole life keeping everyone happy—their parents, the locals who relied on the resorts for their economy, the tourist industry. She'd spent her entire adult working life at the resort juggling all these responsibilities.

And, if she wasn't careful, she was going to crack up under the pressure.

'Shh,' Luke said, his arm tightening around her waist as he absently kissed her neck. 'Shh.'

Claudia cried harder then. It felt so good to have him here. To lean against him for a while. To feel his lips brushing against her neck as he assured her over and over he was here. *Right here*. She felt as if she'd been juggling so many things alone for so long, trying to make the place a viable concern. Trying to be true to their parents' vision and prove to him it could be done.

And it was nice that he didn't say anything else, didn't try and fix things so she'd stop crying. Throw out some trite words about her being strong and how *she could do it*. Because deep down she knew she was strong; she knew she could do it. She was just having an extraordinarily weak moment, and his being here, putting his arms around her and letting her cry was exactly what she needed.

So she cried. She cried until there were no more tears left and she drifted off to sleep.

CHAPTER THREE

LUKE SLEPT TOO. Unfortunately not the deep, dreamless sleep of the severely jet-lagged. The sleep his body was craving. Whether that was the total chaos his diurnal rhythms had been thrown into or the fact that he was draped around warm, soft woman he wasn't sure. But his sleep was disturbed with fevered images cavorting through his head.

Difficult to understand, impossible to hold onto.

They slipped elusively through his fingers like strands of the silky blonde hair fluttering in and out of his reach.

There was a woman in a long, sheer gown. He was chasing her but she was always too far away to catch, to really see her. She was laughing, the tinkly sound echoing through his dream in time with his heartbeat. Every time he got close to her she'd disappear like mist only to reappear again in the distance.

She was naked under the gown, glimpses of her buttocks, the bare arch of her back and the side swell of her breasts taunting him. He was conscious of his arousal as he gave chase, as his legs pumped towards her, the desire to hold her, to kiss her, drumming through his veins.

His body ached with anticipation, his head spun with desire, his breath rasped and not just from the demands of the chase. She laughed again and he ran faster.

Claudia woke to a whirl of sensation spiralling deep and low inside her and sinking lower still, tingling between her legs and dragging heavy fingers down the backs of her thighs. Her eyelids fluttered open and she blinked, trying to orientate herself through eyes that were gritty, the skin around them simultaneously tight and puffy.

Something weighed heavy across her hip and thighs. And her breast. She was aware of heat at her back and hardness nestled between the cheeks of her bottom as she looked down at the hand no longer at her waist but cupping her breast instead. She froze.

Luke.

His hand moved in a circular motion then, gentle and firm all at once, and her nipple responded with blatant enthusiasm, scrunching tight.

Luke groping her.

Claudia's heart thundered behind her ribcage and echoed like gunshots through her ears. She was surprised he couldn't feel it considering how closely acquainted he was becoming with that area of her body.

How long had it been there?

Long enough to have her belly twisted into knots!

She raised her head and looked over her shoulder. He was sound asleep, his leg thrown carelessly over her hip, his thigh trapping hers, weighing her down. His mouth was still at her neck where she remembered it, his hips well and truly aligned with hers and about as close as was humanly possible with clothes on.

She watched as a frown flitted across his forehead, then stared at the stubble covering his jaw, a little darker now. It was surprisingly sexy and Claudia took a slow steady breath to expel any thoughts of sexy from her brain.

She was worried if she moved a hair, a single muscle, if she breathed too deep she would wake him and he'd find himself in this compromising position and then where would that leave them? Their relationship had become fraught enough this past year.

But she needn't have worried. He didn't budge, his body remaining heavy against hers in slumber, effectively trapping her slighter frame.

He wasn't waking and she wasn't going anywhere.

She turned away from him then, slowly placing her head back on her pillow and shutting her eyes. Willing herself not to think about the press of him along the length of her. About the wild tango her hormones were performing. About the persistent tug down low morphing into something else. Something more.

She just revelled for a moment. *This* was how it would feel to be with Luke. To be cherished by him. Comforted. Protected. *Loved.*

This was what she'd fantasised about during all her teen years. Hoping he'd see her as more than the little sister he never had. Hoping he'd kiss her, look at her as if she was a woman rather than a child, take her to his bed.

Hoping he'd stay.

He shifted against her slightly and Claudia held her breath. She expelled it on a quiet whimper as the delicious friction between their bodies ramped up another notch. The roughness of his barely there stubble scraped at the sensitive patch of skin where shoulder met nape and sensation prickled from the point of contact right down to her nipples, tightening them.

His hand squeezed in some kind of subconscious response because he was definitely still heavily asleep. Claudia's eyes practically rolled back in her head as her nipple blazed with hot, fiery need. She pushed back slightly, trying to ease the ache between her legs.

Oh, God. She swallowed. She should move—now! She should get the hell away. She *should not* be using his unsuspecting body as some kind of scratching pole!

Her resort had been declared a disaster zone and Luke was only here for a week.

But neither of those things seemed to matter right now.

She just wanted to push back a little more. Maybe rub herself against him a little. Arch her back, slide her arm up around his neck, pull his mouth down on hers.

Or maybe she could just roll over and press her mouth to his. Beg him for just one time in his arms.

Once was all she needed.

And then her mobile rang.

Luke could hear the chiming of a bell and the woman from his dream faded from sight altogether as his subconscious pulled him back through the layers of sleep.

He came out slowly, groggily, completely disorientated, his brain cells still heavily mired in fatigue. The sunny room wasn't remotely familiar, the ocean sounds weren't familiar, the smell of salt and apple blossom weren't familiar.

He shifted slightly, struggling out from the steely tendrils of his dream. Where were the heavy blackout curtains, the traffic noise, the smell of percolating coffee?

None of it was familiar.

The weight of something warm and distinctly female filled his hand and he squeezed tentatively.

The breast was *definitely* not familiar. The last time he'd woken to a woman in his bed it had been his wife and she washed her hair with expensive shampoo that smelled like designer perfume, not sweet and fresh like apples.

He pulled away, his hand releasing the breast, his leg sliding off the woman's thighs as it all came rushing back.

'Claude?'

Claudia lay frozen for a few seconds; her phone blaring out 'Summer Nights' from *Grease* alerted her to the fact it was Avery calling. Her friend was probably wondering where the hell she'd got to.

Just lying on my bed letting Luke grope me in his sleep. Sheesh!

Claudia didn't answer him or even look back as she snatched up the phone and scrambled off the bed, keeping her back firmly turned on Luke.

'Hi, Avery,' she said chirpily as she picked up the call.

Luke half sat in the bed, his eyes on her back as the memory of Claudia's—*Claude's!*—breast, her very erect nipple, burnt a hole in his palm. He might have been only semi-awake but he'd been fully aware of its arousal, and that was going to be impossible to forget. Especially with his hard-on pressing insistently against the zipper of his trousers. He wanted desperately to adjust it but there was no way he was touching himself with her right there—back turned or not.

He slid off the bed on the opposite side, not really paying any attention to what Avery and Claude were talking about. He needed some space. Some distance.

For adjusting.

For thinking.

For mental flagellation.

Luke stalked to the open balcony door and stepped grate-fully through the curtains and out into the sunshine, easing things inside his underwear as best he could. The harsh sun-light blinded him a little and he squinted against it, raising his arm to block it out.

The ocean was still flat and listless, swishing quietly against the sand, and he took several deep breaths of salty air, filling his lungs with sand and ocean, cleansing it of London smog, wishing it were as easy to cleanse his brain. Erase the mem-ory of Claudia all warm and soft, her nipple stiff and ready.

He turned his back to the vista, the brightness too much for his tired eyes. He shut them but then the edges of his dream fluttered seductively in the periphery of his mind and his eyes snapped open as his erection surged again.

Crap.

What had he done?

He shook his head. No. He'd been having a normal male physiological response to an erotic dream and Claudia just happened to be in the wrong place at the wrong time.

Nothing more, nothing less.

For God's sake, they'd grown up practically siblings.

She was like the kid sister he'd never had. Following him around. Getting into all kinds of mischief and strife with him. Sometimes bratty, always devoted. There'd never been *anything* between them.

He'd *never* felt *anything* other than brotherly towards her.

Except the heat in his palm didn't feel very brotherly. The memory of her softness, *of her hardness*, felt pretty damn carnal.

Which begged the question—why *hadn't* they ever got together? Never had a fling? Never even shared a quick teenage pash? It made sense with their proximity. Of course, she'd been sixteen and he'd been twenty-one when he'd left over eleven years ago but there'd been plenty of times since.

Hell, the only time they'd kissed that didn't revolve around a hello/goodbye was on New Year's Eve—and that had never been anything other than a quick chaste peck on the cheek.

'I have to go,' Claudia said, stepping briskly out on the balcony in a very businesslike manner, tucking her shirt into her awful polyester capris. But Luke wasn't fooled. She forgot he knew her better than anyone and she was as flummoxed as he was about the whole *groping* situation.

'I'm sorry…about before,' he said. Luke knew there was only one way to really deal with what had occurred on her bed.

The same way he dealt with everything.

Head-on.

'Oh…don't worry about it,' Claudia dismissed, looking at the balcony tiles and nervously pulling at the wisps of her hair at the nape of her neck. 'It was nothing.'

'It was not nothing, Claude. It was not my intention to… molest you in my sleep when I crashed in the bed with you. I don't think I can be held entirely accountable for my actions given that I wasn't aware of what I was doing, but I believe in taking responsibility so…I apologise.'

Claudia peeked up at him through her fringe and gave him a vigorous nod. 'Right…yes…good,' she said. 'Now do you think we could never speak of it again?'

Luke laughed then. He'd forgotten how endearingly funny Claudia could be. 'Deal,' he said and stuck out his hand.

She shot him a nervous-looking smile but returned the nice firm grip and he lingered for a moment longer than he would normally have. 'Why didn't we ever...?'

Claudia frowned. 'What?'

'Why didn't we ever...get it on?'

Claudia pulled her hand from his at the unexpected question. He was so sophisticated now. So different from the boy she'd known. Even the way he spoke had changed. Gone were the broad, flat Aussie vowels. He sounded more cultured now, more anglicised. His voice had taken on a smooth richness that poured over her like thick double cream.

Why hadn't they ever got together? Was he insane?

Because you were never interested, idiot.

But even as she thought it Claudia knew it wasn't that simple. There was more to it than that. Much more. Stuff that had never been spoken but somehow she'd known intuitively.

'Too...complicated.' She shrugged. 'We couldn't have just had a fling where we spent some time together and then went our own separate ways because it wouldn't just be us getting together, would it? It'd be our parents too. And if something happened...'

Luke nodded as she trailed off. 'They'd have to take sides. It could ruin a friendship that's somehow survived twenty years of being in business together.'

And if Luke knew one thing it was how easily work relationships turned to dust, and the long-reaching consequences that could have. He was still paying for the faith he'd put into his.

And he'd vowed to never stick his head in the mouth of that lion ever again.

Claudia shrugged. 'We couldn't do that to them. It wouldn't be fair.'

Luke nodded. She was right. Their parents' friendship was a very good reason why he needed to forget how it felt to have Claudia smooshed up against him. To have touched her breast. Felt it respond. He shut his eyes to block the mental image even as his palm tingled. He turned around, grabbing the railing hard as he stared out over acres of calm ocean.

Hell. He *must* be jet-lagged.

Get a grip, man.

Claudia let her gaze wander over the contours of his back. She supposed he didn't have a tan any more. He used to. Surfing every day with Jonah, he used to go a dark nut-brown. His hair used to be long and shaggy.

And then he'd left.

Claudia dragged her mind back to the present. 'I have to go,' she said. 'Avery needs me. Jonah can take you back to Cairns later if you like. I believe there's an afternoon Qantas flight to Heathrow.'

Luke's shoulders tensed and he counted to ten before he turned back to face her. 'I'm not going anywhere for a week,' he said. 'I'll help with the clean-up as much as I can. You might as well just go on and get used to it.'

Claudia regarded him for a moment. His jaw was rigid and his mouth was set in that obstinate line she remembered so well. She'd forgotten how stubborn he could be. And the reality was, she could ill afford to knock back help.

'Fine,' she said. 'Stay. See if I care. I need every bit of muscle I can get my hands on anyway. But we're doing this my way—do you understand? I,' she said, pointing to herself, 'am the boss. You—' she pointed at him '—are the muscle. Got it?'

Luke suppressed the twitch of his lips at Claudia's Little Miss Bossy Britches act. He nodded without saying a word. He'd never been known as *the muscle* before but it brought a whole new connotation to her dominatrix spiel. She narrowed her eyes suspiciously at his easy capitulation but said nothing before turning on her heel and leaving.

His gaze was drawn to the swagger of her butt in those terrible capris.

Who knew polyester could suddenly seem so enticing?

CHAPTER FOUR

THE NEXT DAY they got the all-clear to start the clean-up and for five long days Claudia and the whole crew worked like Trojans to clear the mountains of debris whirled up, ripped to shreds and dumped back down again by the cyclone.

Five long days from sun up to sun down—picking up, chopping up, loading, dumping and starting all over again. Crashing exhausted into bed each night with aches and pains and blisters galore. Waking early to do all again the next day.

Too busy to do any of the leisure things that could usually be indulged in at a beach resort. Too busy to relax on the beach or go surfing after shift end. Too busy for long, boozy chats late into the night. Too busy to take a day off and go out fishing in one of Jonah's charter boats.

Too damn busy for sure to psychoanalyse a very weird moment that should never have happened. Too busy to question it. Too busy to barely say a dozen words to each other.

But when she shut her eyes, all bets were off and Claudia spent a lot of time fantasising about just where that moment could have gone. If she *had* shifted against him, slid her arm around his neck. If he had kissed her, if he'd pushed his hand under her shirt.

This was what happened when there were unfulfilled sexual fantasies. They just grew and grew in the deep, dark recesses of the imagination until a person could barely sleep from the wondering.

Maybe they should have *got it on* as he'd put it. Done it early, rid it from their systems. Hell, their parents would never have even known if they'd had some wild pash one night down on the beach.

It probably would have been one of those awful, soggy, teeth-clashing kisses. *Probably*. And that would have been that.

Because she sure as hell was spending a lot of her supposed sleep time wondering about a wild pash with Luke now.

Too much bloody time.

On the sixth day Claudia was busy inside, ostensibly going over the strategic plan, plotting their progress, seeing what else had to be done/arranged and making some phone calls to local suppliers.

And it really had started out that way.

But from the reception desk she had a bird's eye view of the pool. The pool that Luke had decided was on his to-do list today. She'd actually put it on Cyrus's list but clearly they'd swapped. So there he was in a pair of boardies. And nothing else.

He didn't have that deep nutty tan any more. Although, he had toasted to a light delicious golden colour even in the short time he'd spent back under the north Queensland sun. His chest was as hairless as she remembered, just a sprinkling around his nipples and a fine trail that arrowed down from his belly button.

All the way down.

Her work largely forgotten, Claudia, her handy clipboard clutched to her chest, watched Luke clear all the large debris that had been dumped in the previously sparkling water of the large resort pool that meandered its way all around the outside of the main building. He stood on the edge and pulled it all out with a large net. From leaf matter to building wreckage to about a zillion dead insects.

There was no sign of the mobile phone he had practically glued to his hip the entire week. Taking phone calls from

London at all hours of the day and night, downing tools while he dealt with whatever matter was deemed urgent enough by the person at the other end to interrupt his week off, then picking up again and getting on with it.

Nope, as he waded into the pool with the hand-held industrial vacuum cleaner the phone was nowhere to be seen. Just Luke and his boardies and a pair of reef shoes to protect him from any glass hazards that could still be lying on the bottom of the pool, hidden by the slightly murky water.

With her occupational health and safety hat on, Claudia was pleased to see Luke being cautious. But that wasn't what was causing her to openly ogle him.

No.

That would be the way water droplets clung to his arms and chest, glistening distractedly. The midday sun shone down on him, sparkling in the droplets, and he was literally dazzling to her eyes.

Claudia swallowed as she watched his broad shoulders and powerful quads get to work, sweeping at the layer of silt and sand on the bottom of the pool.

'Hey.'

Claudia almost jumped out of her skin as Avery's voice sounded right near her ear. 'Do you have to creep around like that?' she protested, pressing her hand to her pounding heart.

Avery frowned. 'What's wrong?'

'Nothing,' Claudia muttered, quickly turning back to the desk.

But it was too late. Avery turned to see what had been holding Claudia's attention. And found it.

Or him, as the case may be.

She grinned. 'Well, well, well,' she teased. 'Were you perving on that gorgeous hunk of man flesh, Miss Claude?'

Claudia refused to look up and give anything away. 'Just checking he was wearing the appropriate shoes. That's an accident waiting to happen,' she fobbed.

Avery grinned again. 'Uh-huh.'

Claudia glanced at her friend sharply. 'I was.'

'Uh-huh.'

Claudia shoved her hand on her hip. 'What the hell is that supposed to mean?' she demanded.

Avery shrugged in that gorgeous retro Hollywood movie star way of hers. 'Nothing. I think it's great that you can't take your eyes off Captain Sexypants.'

Claudia blinked. Only Avery would come up with such a fanciful nickname. 'Captain *Sexypants*?' Of all the... 'Just because you are all loved up, Avery Shaw, does not mean the rest of the world is similarly interested.'

'Uh-huh.'

Avery got that dreamy look in her eyes again—the one that had been an almost permanent fixture on her face since she and Jonah had become an item—and Claudia rolled her eyes, returning her attention to the paperwork in front of her.

'You can tell me, you know, Claude. We've been friends a long time—you know you can talk to me.'

Claudia glanced up as Avery turned serious, her American accent more pronounced when edged with worry. The thing was she knew she could. Or she used to be able to anyway. But then the resort got dumped on her as a sole responsibility and, even though Avery had been there by her side throughout it all, the onus still fell directly on Claudia's shoulders. Trying to keep it altogether, make it all work, had forced Claudia into an almost permanent state of seriousness, with no time for frivolous girly chatter.

And then Avery had hooked up with Jonah and how could Claudia possibly dump her problems on her friend's shoulders? Avery was happy—she didn't want to bother her with trivial stuff.

The days of their girlhood confidences had been well and truly squashed by her very adult responsibilities.

So now she wasn't sure how she could say, well, actually, Avery, Luke sleep-groped me a few days back and I'm so sexually frustrated I think I might die from it or at the very least jump the next guy who walks through the door.

How could she even voice that, think of her own petty desires, when the world around her had gone to hell and there were so much more important things to deal with?

And it was just as well she didn't as Jonah chose that moment to walk through the door and Avery's face lit up as if he were dipped in chocolate and rolled in sugar.

'I know, Avery,' Claudia said, and smiled at her best friend in the whole world. 'I know. I just have a lot on my plate.'

Avery gave her shoulder a squeeze. 'You need a break.'

Claudia nodded. 'Later.' She tapped a pen against the resort plans in front of her. 'After.'

But then Jonah's, 'Where are those refreshments, woman?' boomed across the foyer and Avery said, 'I'm just going to organise some drinks for the workers.'

Claudia nodded absently. ''Kay. See you later.'

Claudia watched as Avery took off in Jonah's direction and smiled as Jonah swept her up and pressed a very indecent kiss on Avery's mouth. She looked away.

Outside. To the pool.

Luke was boosting himself up on the side, his back to her. Water sluiced off his hair and down over his shoulders and the perfectly delineated muscles of his back. For a man who had an office job, he was in excellent shape. In one smooth movement he'd twisted and sat on the coping of the pool. The broad expanse of his chest was exposed to her view now and Claudia drank it in. Firm pecs, flat abs and that distinct trail of hair that arrowed from his belly button down...

Before she could follow it all the way to its destination, Luke turned again and pushed up through powerful quads into a standing position.

Her gaze was drawn to those legs. Lightly haired, his calves firm without being bulky. And then there were his boardies. His *very wet boardies* that clung in all the wrong places, outlining the hardness of quads beneath but also the part of his anatomy she'd felt up close and personal only days before.

Claudia's mouth suddenly felt as dry as day-old toast.

He chose that moment to look up and suddenly she was looking straight into his eyes. Eyes that, despite distance and the barrier of glass, seemed to pierce right to her centre. Their gazes locked and held and Claudia's heart banged around in her chest. Her breath hitched. Her mouth went from dry to arid.

There was a frankness to his gaze and in that instant she knew, *she just knew*, he'd been aware of her interest all along. A part of her wanted to hide behind the desk, hide from the directness in his gaze, but he chose that moment to sweep a flat palm up his belly to his chest and her eyes helplessly followed.

She couldn't look away.

He motioned to her then, inviting her to join him and, God help her, she wanted to. *Really freaking bad.*

But the phone rang, dragging her back from the edge, and she leapt on it as if it were the last life buoy left on a sinking ship, picking it up and brandishing it at him, barely stopping herself from kissing it.

He looked at her long and hard for a moment before shrugging and nodding and she turned away gratefully, catching her breath as she greeted the caller, her usual chipper phone manner lost in the mental images of a half-naked Luke.

Captain Sexypants indeed.

Later that evening, with the bulk of the clean-up finally completed, Claudia threw an impromptu luau down on the beach for all the volunteers. Back before the resort was blown to hell, every Saturday night was luau night. It was one of their most popular themed events amongst their largely family clientele as well as Crescent Cove locals.

This wasn't going to be anywhere near as fancy as that.

There wouldn't be drums and ukuleles to hula to and there wouldn't be the usual feast but then, there wouldn't be two hundred people either. There was only a dozen to cater for and, given that there was enough raw material to make a bonfire big enough to be seen from space, all they really needed was some fresh seafood and some cold drinks.

Jonah had been tasked with taking one of his boats out and catching some fish, which he'd done most admirably. Tony, their chef, who was still with them after all these years, had cooked the fish along with an amazing rice-in-coconut-milk concoction and piping-hot fresh bread. Avery had dug out the leis and a CD of Hawaiian music.

And even if partying was the last thing Claudia and her aching body felt like, she put on her uniform, plastered a smile on her face and was the chipper Claude that everyone knew and loved because these people had helped out and worked like dogs, out of the goodness of their hearts, and she owed them.

But it felt good to sit down on one of the logs that ringed the fire and just listen to the chatter and the swish of the ocean. To not do anything. It felt like the first time she'd sat and done nothing for over a week.

She buried her toes in the cool sand and let the bliss take over. Hull, Jonah's hulking great hound, had collapsed on the sand beside her.

She tipped her head from side to side to stretch out aching neck muscles. She rubbed at the left side with her hand and winced as her index finger twinged. She looked down at her hands. They were in bad shape from a week of hard labour—some old blisters on her palms in various stages of healing, her fingers rough and dry from pulling out a zillion splinters.

She'd kill for a day at one of those fancy spas.

Iron out the kinks with a massage. Get a pedicure. Sit in a sauna and soak half the day. Maybe one of those full-body scrubs.

Nearby laughter pulled her out of her fantasy and Claudia smiled as she watched Cyrus and Isis perform a rather good hula. Jonah in his boardies and Avery in a tangerine bikini with a matching sarong low on her hips danced a much closer, sexier number in the shadows further away, lost in each other.

A pang of jealousy bit Claudia hard in the chest.

'They look good together.'

Claudia looked up, all the way up, to find Luke looking down at her. He was in boardies as well—dry this time, *thank goodness*—and his chest was covered with a form-fitting T-shirt. She resolutely ignored the wetter, less dressed image of him that floated in her mind's eye but his eyebrow kicked up and he looked at her as if he knew exactly what she was thinking.

'Yes, they do,' she said and hoped like hell the words didn't sound as squeaky as they'd felt leaving her throat.

She was relieved when he broke eye contact, handing her a frosty bottle of beer. She took it gratefully as he stepped over the log and lowered his butt, plonking down beside her.

Claudia shifted to make some room for him.

Or put some space between them, anyway.

She looked back at the fire, which had settled from a blazing inferno to a dull roar, as they both took some swallows of their beers, neither saying anything for a few moments. Until Luke mentioned the elephant sitting next to them at the fire.

'I was hoping you'd join me in the pool today. Just like old times.' Luke had been acutely aware of her eyes on him today and his blood had flowed thick and sludgy through his veins as her gaze had continued to linger.

Claudia kept her eyes firmly fixed on the flames that danced before her. Why had he hoped that? Surely after a sleepy grope he knew they'd progressed far beyond the innocent pool games they'd played as kids? Even through the glass of the window she'd felt the pull of him, had been aware of him like no other man.

'I don't do much swimming these days,' she dismissed.

'What, not even in that magnificent ocean right on your doorstep?'

She shook her head. 'Too busy.'

Luke took a swig of his beer 'That's a shame...I seem to remember you looked good in a bikini.'

Claudia faltered, her pulse flickering madly in time with the flame as she glanced at him. What was she supposed to say to that? *Since when did you pay any attention to how I looked in a bikini? Or, not as good as you do in wet clingy boardies?*

Or maybe, more aptly, *don't flirt with me*?

'I leave the bikinis to Avery,' she said, dropping her gaze to the fire again. 'There's too much to do at the moment to bunk off for a cool dip.'

Luke tutted at her dismissal. 'The clean-up's essentially done,' Luke said. 'I'm sure you could have squeezed in a quick, dirty swim.'

Claudia, who almost choked on her beer, was shocked into looking at him again. He laughed at her scandalised look, then winked. 'I was referring to the state of the water.'

She narrowed her eyes at him, wondering how many beers he'd consumed. Maybe the jet lag was hitting him in one large wallop and taking over his mouth.

Either way, she chose to ignore his comment and the direction he seemed to want to steer the conversation. 'The outside is largely complete but there's still a long way to go,' she said. 'We have to keep moving forward.'

Luke sighed at her determination to stay serious. He'd hoped as he'd sat beside her that she'd loosen up a little— relax as everyone else was doing.

But no. The uniform should have been a clue.

'So what's next?' he asked as he reached down and absently petted a mellow Hull.

Claudia took a mouthful of her beer before she answered.

'Back to the drawing board. Starting again. Working out how much I can do with the insurance money.'

'It's not going to cover it all?'

Claudia shook her head. 'It may have been enough twenty years ago, not today. Hell, it'd probably have been enough for just a normal cyclone but…'

Luke took a swig of his drink and watched Claudia's toes, painted a cute shade of pink, wiggle in the sand.

'So you want to talk about where we go from here?'

He felt her tense beside him and her toes stopped their wriggling. 'I'm not selling to some consortium, some…giant hotel chain, Luke.' She glared at him and Luke couldn't decide if the flare in her eyes came from her sudden well of pissed off, or the fire.

'If you've stopped by to butter me up about that you might as well keep on going.'

Luke knew it was important to stay calm and frankly he was too wrecked from a week of hard yakka to get into an argument. 'Okay, so what *are* we going to do?'

'The Tropicana has been here for forty years. *Our parents* ran it together for twenty of those years. And it will be again.'

'Complete with Tiki Suites, salsa nights and lei stringing?'

Luke felt her hostile glance shoot bullets of disapproval straight into his chest.

'Yes. What's wrong with those things?' she demanded. 'I know they probably don't seem very sophisticated to Mr Hotshot Ad Exec, but the Tropicana has always been a family resort—that's the way our parents wanted it. And that's the way it's going to stay.'

'And what about *you*, Claude? What do *you* want?'

Claudia frowned. Where was the man who had teased her about a bikini before? He was looking at her as he had by the pool earlier, as if he was trying to see all the way to the inside. And now, as then, it discomforted her.

'What do you mean?'

'I mean if you were given a bottomless bucket of money and told you could build whatever you wanted—*anything*—what would you build? Not what our parents wanted, not what the town wants, not what's always been. What Claudia Davis wants.'

Luke watched her intently as she opened her mouth to say something and then shut it again. Conflict crinkled her brow. Wisps of blonde hair had loosened from her ponytail and the ocean breeze blew them gently across her face. The firelight played across her features complementing their fineness but it also illuminated her internal struggle, backlit her doubt.

She chewed on her bottom lip, contemplating the question as if he'd just asked her to tell him the meaning of life in ten words or less. The firelight glowed in the moisture she was creating and his gaze dropped to her mouth briefly before returning to the fire, tuning into the background noises of surf, laughter and hula music.

He drank his beer and waited quietly for her to figure it out. Was the question really that difficult?

Claudia contemplated the rim of her beer bottle, conscious of the time ticking away. She didn't know. She'd been so caught up in her parents' vision it had become her own. And she loved the kitschy, retro feel they'd created. But *was* it what she wanted?

What *did* she want?

She rubbed absently at her neck again and the muscles protested. 'A day spa,' she said on a whim. 'A place for people to be pampered.'

Luke blinked, both surprised and excited by her answer. 'Yeah?'

For a brief moment their eyes met and the spark in his caused a flutter of possibility inside Claudia's chest. But reality intruded and snuffed it out. She shook her head. 'The people we attract here can't afford that kind of decadence, Luke. We're the affordable alternative.'

'Can't we be both?'

Claudia frowned. 'Being good at one thing is better than being half-arsed at two.'

'So then let's not be half-arsed. Let's be some kind of hybrid resort where we cater to both ends of the market.'

'I think that'll be really confusing to the market, don't you? High-ticket clients aren't going to want to be bothered by a bunch of screaming kids and salsa lessons on the beach.'

Luke shrugged. 'So we keep them separate—we have enough land. Why shut ourselves off to another, potentially very lucrative, source of income?'

Claudia could feel that flutter again and her pulse picked up slightly as her imagination started to run a little wild. Avery would be great at managing and running a spa business. Temptation shimmied possibilities in front of her— typical that Luke would be an integral part of that, enticing her with firelight and his strange but lovely accent like a big, fat, juicy apple.

She dragged her gaze off him and looked into the fire. Bad enough that he'd reminded her of how she'd perved on him in the pool today, but now he was waving a shiny new future in front of her.

Get behind me, Satan.

Luke was encouraged by Claudia's contemplation, the little flare of interest he'd seen in her gaze. He nudged his thigh against hers and a quiver of something hot and sinful spread all the way up to his groin. 'Just think about it, Claude. You don't have to rush into anything.'

Claudia looked down at his thigh, all warm and muscled in the firelight. And tempting. Oh, so tempting. It was hot against hers and she didn't think it had anything to do with the fire. Did he feel it too or was it just her? She wondered what he'd do if she slid her hand onto it. If she slowly moved it upwards.

Right. To. The. Top.

She blinked as the image formed in real time in her head

and stood abruptly, shocked by the ferocity of the urge to follow through. 'I'll think about it,' she said, looking straight ahead. Not down at him. And his eyes. And his smile.

And his outrageously sexy accent.

Luke smiled at the stiffness of her stance. 'Good,' he murmured.

Claudia nodded. 'Right, well…I think I might turn in,' she said, still not looking at him.

Luke chuckled. 'Sweet dreams.'

Claudia swallowed as she thought about the dreams she'd been having this last week.

Not one of them sweet.

'See you in the morning,' she said with as much nonchalance as she could muster before she fled the beach for the safety of the Copacabana Suite, far away from men with sexy accents and delectable thighs.

CHAPTER FIVE

CLAUDIA BARELY SLEPT a wink. It was as if Luke had tripped some switch in her brain and a hundred different possibilities for what the Tropicana *could* be had bombarded her. And frankly it was a relief to think about something other than the way Luke's hand had felt on her breast. The way his boardies had clung to him in the pool.

The way his thigh had sizzled against hers.

By the time morning rocked around, her head was buzzing. And she needed to share! Avery and Jonah weren't on her radar—she'd walked in on them too many times to know that spontaneous bursts of shared creativity were off the table.

But the one man who had inspired them was just through a connecting door and he was in there alone.

She rose at six, climbed into her uniform—the skirt for a change—and made copious notes. When she was all spent she took to the floor, pacing it until the clock ticked over to seven—a perfectly reasonable hour. After that, all propriety was off. She rapped once on the door before pushing it open, knowing in her gut that Luke wouldn't have locked it.

The room was like a black hole when she pressed inside but that didn't deter her. It was only eight in the evening in the UK—still a perfectly decent hour. She marched over to the curtains from familiarity alone and yanked them back with a harsh squeal along the railing. Another impossibly sunny day greeted her and was surprisingly buoying.

Luke's eyes scrunched up as he stirred. He rolled on his side and prised open an eyelid to check the time on the clock beside his bed. 'What the hell?' he groaned, rolling on his back, knowing it was Claudia in his room without having to sight her. 'There better be another cyclone on the horizon,' he griped, 'because I thought this was our day of rest.'

'Sorry,' Claudia chirped although she didn't sound very sorry at all.

'Shut the curtain,' Luke said. 'Nowhere has the right to be this bright so early.'

'You're such a city boy now,' she scoffed as she acquiesced and closed half the curtain.

'I'm still on London time,' he protested.

'Whatever, city boy,' Claudia dismissed. 'Wake up. I've been up all night and it's all your fault.'

At another time, when he wasn't exhausted from hard physical labour and the remnants of jet lag, Luke might have taken that as a compliment. Might have raised his eyebrow and shot her a little *oh, really* look. But he was having trouble prising his eyes open.

And this was Claude. He didn't think about Claude in that context. *Or he never used to anyway...* Thinking about keeping her up at night was just plain wrong.

'Come back in an hour and tell me then,' he muttered, rolling on his side and plonking a pillow over his head.

Claudia glared at his covered head. 'Hey,' she protested, marching to his side and whisking the offending pillow away, tossing it on the ground. 'I know you're flying back to London tomorrow but I have ideas. Lots of ideas.'

Luke groaned. So did he. None of them sane. All of them X-rated. But she looked very awake. Very no-nonsense. Very determined. He sighed, resigning himself to his fate, pushing himself up into a semi-upright position against the head of the bed, his hands rubbing at his eyes.

'Okay, fine,' he said when he could just make her out through bleary eyes tortured by the kind of sunlight he'd never been privy to in his ten plus years in London. How quickly eyeballs forgot!

Then of course they were subjected to further torture by Claudia standing at the end of his bed in that horrendous uniform that somehow seemed to get sexier the more he saw her in it.

'What have you got?' he demanded with a gruffness that he was fairly sure had some kind of sexual genesis.

Claudia narrowed her eyes. He didn't look very awake. 'Do you need coffee?' she demanded.

Luke snorted. There were about a hundred things he needed, including dragging her into bed and stripping her out of her awful clothes, pulling out that damn ponytail and kissing her till she stopped growling and started purring.

Coffee didn't even rate.

Clearly his sanity was of much greater concern.

'Just speak,' he griped. '*You* woke me. And now I'm vertical and reasonably awake. So speak.'

Claudia tsked. 'I remember a time when you would have been up and on your surfboard catching a wave somewhere by now.'

'Claude.'

The warning in his voice told Claudia she'd stretched his patience long enough and she opened her mouth, prepared to get down to business, to launch into her spiel, and then his state of dress registered. Or, undress, to be exact. He was sitting up looking all big and broad with a very naked chest leading to a very naked abdomen and that very, very nice happy trail meandering downwards to what she began to suspect might be a very naked everything else.

'Are you…wearing *any* clothes?'

Luke looked at her for long moments and didn't answer and Claudia wished she could bite her tongue off. She hadn't meant to voice her concerns but she was so used to speaking her mind around him she'd forgotten that they were all grown up now. That some things just weren't said.

'No. I always sleep naked. Why? Don't you?'

Claudia snorted. 'No.'

'What, not even after sex?'

Heat rose in Claudia's cheeks. She really didn't want to discuss her sexual habits with Luke. 'That's none of your damn business.'

Luke couldn't agree more. Thinking about sex and Claudia in the buff were not places he wanted his mind to wander.

Clearly he needed more asleep

'You're right,' he sighed. 'I apologise. Now can we please just get this over with?'

Claudia folded her arms across her chest as she stared at his. 'I'd really prefer you to not be naked when I'm talking to you.'

And he'd prefer her to be a lot more naked than she was. Irritation needled him. 'Well, we don't always get what we want.'

Claudia dragged her gaze up. Fine. Tiredness was making him belligerent. She'd show him she could be cool about talking to a naked man. Who was in bed. With bed hair. And a shadowy hint of stubble along his jawline.

She wasn't some middle-aged prude. She was perfectly fine with nudity.

And bed hair. And stubble.

Luke rubbed his hand over his jaw, the rasp loud in the silence. He needed a shave. After some more sleep. 'Claude, I swear if you don't say something I'm just going to go to sleep sitting up.'

Claudia nodded. Speaking. She could do that. She cleared her throat. 'I was thinking about...' His bare chest was distracting in her peripheral vision. 'The whole spa idea. About...' He rubbed at his jaw again and the rasp went straight to her nipples. They tightened in blatant response, almost as if he'd scraped his chin over the sensitive tips, and she was thankful for the palm-tree pattern disguising their reaction.

Dear Lord, where was she? She cleared her throat again. 'Catering to that end of the market.'

'Yes?'

His slight accent dragged sticky fingers across her belly and she absently placed her hand on her midriff, pressing slightly to relieve the tingle. 'I was thinking about how we could offer the spa customers a fuller service, including exclusive accommodation. Have you seen those deluxe tents with four-poster beds that sit on raised wooden floorboards and are draped in the most luxurious georgette screening? They open to the ocean and look like something out of *Arabian Nights*?'

Luke knew the type Claudia was talking about—one of his clients dealt exclusively in that style of accommodation—but her hand resting where it was had become very distracting. Her fingers drummed against her belly as she spoke and he was beginning to have very bad thoughts indeed.

Which was not conducive to his nakedness.

Also, *this was Claudia!*

He pulled his legs up, tenting the sheet. 'I think it sounds perfect for the Tropicana—we have enough land to make it a really exclusive set-up.'

Claudia nodded, temporarily forgetting in her enthusiasm Luke was wearing nothing but a sheet. She even took a step towards his bed and propped her knee on the end of the mattress. 'If we set it up right the two parts of the resort could be kept separate but co-exist quite happily.'

Luke chuckled as Claudia's blue eyes shone like polished topaz. 'You look exactly like you used to on Christmas Eve,' he teased.

Claudia smiled back. 'I can't remember being this excited about anything since that Christmas I got that amazing bike from Santa but I was more interested in the clipboard your parents gave me. Do you remember? I think I was ten.'

His smile broadened into a grin at the memory. It must have cost his parents next to nothing but she'd loved that damn thing. 'And you walked around pretending you were Julie from *The Love Boat*.' He laughed.

'And hardly ever rode the bike,' Claudia said, laughing too.

They laughed together for a while until it petered out and the intimacy of the situation invaded again. They were alone in Luke's room and one of them was naked.

Claudia withdrew her knee from the bed. 'Anyway... sorry for waking you, I just...'

Luke waved her apology away with his hand. 'You're forgiven. Just make sure you bring coffee next time.'

'What makes you think there'll be a next time?'

'You mean you're *not* going to make a habit of barging into my room at ungodly hours?'

Claudia rolled her eyes. 'It's seven. And you're leaving tomorrow, remember?'

'I'm still on holiday today.'

'Some holiday,' she snorted. And then they were grinning at each other again.

'Get out of here,' Luke said as their grins faded.

Claudia crossed her arms again. 'You're not going back to sleep, are you?'

'Nope. I'm getting out of bed and hitting the shower. I just figured you wouldn't want to be here when I peeled this sheet back.'

Claudia couldn't help herself—her gaze dropped to the sheet covering his tented knees. Suddenly the familiar easiness between them evaporated and a more loaded atmosphere took over.

'Right. No,' she said, willing her legs to move, but somehow remained rooted to the spot. 'That would be...too much information.'

Luke chuckled at her understatement. 'Amongst other things.' He waited for her to move and chuckled again when she remained stationary. 'Claude?'

Claudia sprang into action this time, embarrassed by her inertia. 'Right. Yes,' she said, pulling down the hem of her skirt a little and brushing imaginary lint from her sleeves. 'I'll just...I'll catch you...later.'

She didn't wait for his reply and two seconds later Luke was practically staring at her dust. He fell sideways onto the mattress with a groan.

He didn't like this...*vibe*...between them now. He and Claude just didn't do vibes.

It would be good to go home tomorrow. Put some distance between them and get back to his job, to a career that was finally on the up again. Especially now Claudia and he were on the same page for the direction of the resort.

An image of Claudia's fingers drumming against her belly slid into his mind.

He reached for a pillow and pulled it over his head. Tomorrow couldn't come soon enough.

'Surprise!' Avery said as Claudia entered the large bright dining room populated with potted palms and an underwater-world mural taking up one entire wall. She couldn't get used to seeing it so empty, bereft of the usual bustling morning breakfast crowd.

Both her and Luke's parents grinned at her from a nearby table.

Claudia almost dropped her clipboard at the sight. She'd told them not to dare cut their big adventure short, that there was nothing they could do here anyway. When the cyclone had been building and finally hit, the intrepid adventurers had been out of reach on safari somewhere in the Great Sandy Desert and hadn't even been aware. But as soon as they'd returned to civilisation and seen the news they'd been on to Claudia.

They'd insisted on coming home but Claudia had begged them not to. She didn't need to worry about four grey nomads driving a massive RV at breakneck speed, especially when they were over five thousand kilometres away and the roads were still a treacherous mess.

But damn...it was good to see them.

An immediate lump lodged in her throat and she forced it

down—she'd done her crying. No more tears. 'Mum? Dad? When did the road open?'

'This morning.' Lena, her mother, smiled.

'You didn't have to come,' she said. 'We're managing.'

'We know. But we couldn't not.'

And then she was swept into their arms and there were hugs all round and everyone talking at once. The whole disaster and clean-up was retold as Tony served breakfast then sat at the table and ate with them, adding his own embellishments about the worst storm he'd seen in all his forty years.

'Where's Luke?' Gloria, his mother, asked. 'He's not still asleep, is he? It's not like him to lie in.'

'I think the jet lag's really knocking him around,' Avery said.

'We've been working him pretty hard. Getting those soft office hands all dirty.' Jonah grinned.

Cyrus, Tony and Brian, Luke's father, laughed. 'He should be down soon,' Claudia interrupted. 'He was getting up to have a shower when I left him.'

The table fell instantly silent and every set of eyes swivelled to her. It took a moment for Claudia to figure out why until she glanced at Avery's huge goggle eyes.

'Oh…not like that,' she said hurriedly. 'I was just telling him about my ideas for the resort. I thought he was an early riser too. I didn't think he'd be asleep when I went through the connecting door.'

More silence. 'He was asleep?' Gloria finally asked.

'Like a log,' Claudia confirmed.

Luke's parents looked at each other and Claudia was struck as per usual by how Luke was a perfect combination of both of them. His father's build, his mother's brown eyes and gorgeous complexion. 'Does he still sleep in the buff?' Brian asked.

Claudia averted her gaze as a tide of heat rose to her cheeks, missing the wink Brian shot Jonah. 'Apparently,' she said, forcing her voice to sound normal and not crack as she thought about those abs.

That happy trail.

She glanced at Avery, preferring not to be looking at Brian as she thought about his almost naked son. Brian who was very much the blueprint for Luke. Avery was sharing a loaded look with Gloria.

'He's leaving on the evening plane tomorrow,' she blurted out. Claudia wasn't exactly sure why she'd said it but it seemed important for them all to know that Luke wasn't part of the Tropicana equation.

Wasn't part of *her* equation.

'Well, that's a shame,' Gloria said.

Claudia couldn't agree more but for some strange reason she felt compelled to defend him. 'His career is important to him.'

Gloria patted Claudia's hand. 'Yes, dear, we know. Now...' she picked up her cup of tea '...tell us about these plans you were discussing with Luke.'

Pleased for the change in subject, Claudia launched into her spiel with enthusiasm. There was so much she didn't know yet, so much she still had to figure out, but she couldn't deny the excitement that fizzed through her veins.

The last year or so she'd felt as if she'd been going through the motions. Sure, she loved the Tropicana *unconditionally*, had never thought to change a single thing, but now change had been forced upon her whether she liked it or not.

It had been a revelation realising that she'd never been particularly challenged here—she could do what she did in her sleep with her clipboard tied behind her back.

It had been a revelation realising that she *wanted* change.

Still, she was nervous. Ownership of the resort wasn't hers—their parents had just handed over management rights. She had to convince them. Get them on board.

Their enthusiastic nodding helped put her mind at ease. Avery was over-the-moon excited.

'And Luke supports this too?' Gloria asked.

'He sure does,' came a voice from behind them.

Claudia watched as first his parents then her parents embraced Luke. It was heartening to see how close he was with her family too. He was wearing another pair of boardies and a T-shirt and the hem lifted a little to reveal a peek of those smooth abs she'd seen in full Technicolor not that long ago. She dragged her gaze away.

When the greetings were finally done he pulled up the chair beside her and gave her a smile. 'It's like a family reunion,' he said.

Claudia smiled back, forgetting the abs for a moment. It had been a long time since they'd all sat down to a meal together and she felt strangely nostalgic.

'So you're leaving tomorrow?' Lena, Claudia's mum, asked. She was petite and blonde like her daughter and always cut straight to the chase.

Luke nodded. 'No need for me to stick around. The cleanup is largely done and Claude and I are both on the same page with the direction of the resort. I can leave it in her very capable hands and we can communicate via email.'

Luke didn't notice the look his mother and Claudia's mother shared with Avery. He was tucking into the bacon that Tony was renowned for. Claudia didn't either. She was trying to not think about eating bacon off Luke's abs.

CHAPTER SIX

By the end of the day Claudia had almost burned through their entire download quota as she madly surfed the net for any information on spas and the kind of exclusive accommodation and experience she had in mind for the new and improved Tropicana. Thank goodness the web was up and running after a week without.

She and Luke talked extensively, working together in the brief time they had left to throw ideas around, and she made copious notes. She refused to dwell on the fact that he'd be gone tomorrow, that the resort still meant so little to him that he could just walk away, especially after it had been so devastated. If anything the disaster that had befallen the Tropicana had only brought her closer to the grand old dame.

This was where she belonged. Right here.

Walking away just wasn't an option.

Occasionally Claudia glanced up to find her and Luke's mothers in a huddle with their fathers or with Avery or with Avery and Jonah. Sometimes with Isis and Cyrus involved. Even Tony had come out of the kitchen at one point. But she figured they had a lot of catching up to do and everyone was still going about their assigned chores so who was she to complain?

It wasn't until they were sitting around eating their evening meal that night that she began to suspect there was more at play.

'You two were very busy today,' her mother murmured, flicking her glance over them both.

'Lots to plan.' Claudia shrugged.

'How soon do you think you can get started?' her father asked.

'Not sure, Harry,' Luke said. 'Nothing can really be accomplished until the insurance money comes through. The government and the insurance companies have promised the industry that claims will be processed speedily but...' he shrugged '...that doesn't mean it'll actually happen.'

Her father nodded. 'So it could be quite some months before we're back on the road again.'

Claudia looked up, alarmed. 'No...Mum, Dad.' She reached over and squeezed her mother's hand. 'Brian and Gloria,' she said, looking at them both individually. 'Go back to your trip. You guys slogged your guts out here for twenty years and this is supposed to be your retirement. Your dream trip. We'll be just fine without you, won't we, Avery?'

'Hmm,' Avery said noncommittally, avoiding Claudia's gaze. 'I suppose...'

Claudia frowned at her friend, who'd been wildly enthusiastic this morning, before turning back to face the parents. 'We'll be fine,' she assured.

'Of course you will be, darling,' her mother said, squeezing her hand back. 'But...we can't just leave you to do it on your own. Not with your management partner heading back to London. That wouldn't be fair.'

Claudia glanced at Luke. She wished he weren't leaving but the truth was she'd managed without him for over a year and she wasn't going to pressure him into staying.

'I'm not on my own. I have Avery.' Claudia glanced at her friend, who wasn't looking so confident all of a sudden. Maybe she was thinking how much time it was going to take away from her relationship with Jonah?

'We turned the resort around last year,' she said. 'We can rebuild it.'

'No.' Her mother shook her head. 'We'll have to stay. We can't just abandon you. Rebuilding is different from refurbishing—it's a much bigger undertaking. No,' she declared again with a determined shake of her head. 'With Luke gone we'll stay as long as it takes to get the resort on its feet again.'

Luke's mother nodded wildly in agreement. 'Of course, we really don't know anything about the kind of high-end stuff you're talking about doing so we may have to…modify some of the things you were talking about. I mean, the Tropicana clientele really don't expect to be pampered like that when they're here with their kiddies. I'm not sure we should be so…exclusive. We don't want to put anyone off.'

Claudia could feel it all unravelling as Gloria and her mother nodded in unison. She glanced at Luke to find the same kind of alarm written all over his face.

'We're hoping to attract a different clientele,' Luke said through a forced smile.

'Well, of course, darling,' Gloria said. 'But it's not really the spirit of the Tropicana, is it?'

'I agree,' Harry said. 'One of the resort's charms is that it's not pretentious.'

'And surely the objective is to get the place up and running as soon as possible?' Gloria added. 'We can do that blindfolded if we keep it the way it was. Creating this whole new…concept will add a lot of burden to the process.'

'I think your mother's right,' Brian said, sliding his hand on top of Gloria's. 'I think the resort is a little too old to be changing its spots now. It's increasingly difficult to attract the tourist dollar. I surely don't need to tell an ad man that, do I, son? I think if we stay we're better off sticking with the devil we know.'

'I guess we could turn one of the rooms into a massage parlour,' Lena added. 'We could employ some of those lovely commune people down at the markets who offer fifteen-minute neck and shoulder massages. You know how we feel about local employment.'

Claudia watched as her shiny new dreams disappeared slowly into the ether; her shoulders sagged a little. 'Well, of course…it's still your place,' she said carefully. 'We can't do any of it without your support. If you'd prefer we keep it as is…then, of course, that's what we'll do.'

It had been a long shot anyway. Pie-in-the-sky stuff. And their parents were right—why mess with a winning formula?

Luke could feel Claudia's dismay without even having to look at her; it rolled towards him on a heavy cloud of doom. She'd started the day, her eyes sparking with possibility and now she was practically hunched over her untouched meal.

He looked at his parents, then at hers.

They had to go.

In one brief conversation they'd sucked all her joy away.

'Or you could place some faith in us and let us do our thing. Go back to your holiday and trust us,' he said.

'But it won't be *your* thing, will it?' Lena said. The rebuke was gentle but Luke heard it nonetheless. 'You'll be in London and it'll just be poor Claude left to cope and carry all the responsibility. No.' Lena shook her head. 'She's twenty-seven years old—she's too young for that kind of pressure. We're not going to let Claude start from scratch all on her own, not with such a big venture.'

It was on the tip of Luke's tongue to remind them they'd already left her all on her own. But of course they hadn't, had they?

He had.

'Mum, I'm fine,' Claudia dismissed.

Lena smiled at her daughter. 'Of course you are, darling. And you will continue to be so because we're going to be here every step of the way.'

Claudia smiled at her mother wishing she didn't feel suddenly trapped and smothered by their love and thoughtfulness. She'd never felt it before, but then she hadn't had this much freedom before. She'd been running things solo since their parents had taken off and that had been really freeing.

She wasn't sure she wanted to go back.

Claudia's head throbbed at the thought. 'Actually, if no

one minds, I think I'm going to turn in. I've got a bit of a headache.'

'Of course not, darling,' her mother said as Claudia stood. 'Have you got some tablets you can take?'

Claudia nodded. 'Yes…thanks.' She smiled at the group sitting around the table, deliberately avoiding Luke's gaze. 'I'll see you in the morning,' she said.

Luke glared at them all as they watched her go. 'I hope you're all happy now,' he said.

'What on earth do you mean, Luke?' his mother asked.

Luke stood. 'Forget it,' he said, throwing his napkin on the table, and took off after Claudia.

The table waited until Luke had left the dining room before they grinned at each other and Avery leaned across the table and high-fived Gloria.

Luke caught up with Claudia on the stairs. 'Claude, wait,' he said, taking them two at a time. She kept going. 'Claudia,' he called again and she stopped as he caught up with her.

'I'm fine, Luke,' she said wearily. 'Just tired.'

'Fine and dandy, huh?' he mocked.

Claudia didn't deign to answer. She turned away from him and continued up the stairs.

'You should fight for what you want,' he said as he followed a step behind her.

Claudia concentrated on her feet. 'It's their place, Luke.'

'Is that what it is?' he demanded. 'Or are you just too chicken? You've had an original idea that just might turn this giant white elephant of theirs around but you don't have the guts to go for it. You're running scared.'

Claudia stopped as a well of anger rolled through her. She turned abruptly, narrowly avoiding a collision with Luke. Even with him on the lower step he was still taller than her. She clenched her fists to stop herself from placing them on his chest and pushing him down the stairs.

Or possibly tearing his shirt off.

This close she could see every fleck that made up the brown of his eyes, every single eyelash, every individual whisker valiantly trying to push through the skin to freedom before he once again ruthlessly mowed them down.

He couldn't taunt her in that hybrid accent of his—not about this. 'I think you're the only one running around here, Luke.'

And then she turned again and ran up the remaining stairs, putting as much distance between them as possible.

When she got to her room she thanked her lucky stars her parents had decided to take a different room rather than reclaim this one. She didn't fancy sharing with them again—not tonight anyway. And God knew, there were plenty of suites to choose from at the moment!

She didn't turn the light on. She didn't have a shower, she didn't brush her teeth, she didn't even put on her pyjamas. For the first time in her life, Claudia stripped straight out of her clothes and left them discarded on the floor where she stood before walking to the bed, yanking back the sheets and crawling between them.

She sighed as the thick, crisp sheets folded her in cool starched bliss. It felt heavenly even though she knew in this sticky tropical weather she was bound to wake up in a few hours with body parts sticking together. But right now she was just too damn exhausted—physically and mentally—to care.

And hey, if it was good enough for Captain Sexypants...

His outrageous accusation on the stairs came back to her and Claudia shut her eyes to ward it off. She took five deep breaths, tuning in to the gentle swish of the ocean floating to her on a breeze that rustled the balcony curtains. She would not let Luke under her skin. He was leaving tomorrow and things here would return to business as usual.

She shifted around in the king-sized bed trying to get comfortable, not sure this whole naked thing was conducive to sleep.

Sex, maybe, but not sleep.

Hot, sweaty, dirty sex.

She shut her eyes, trying not to think about anything hot, sweaty or dirty or how long it had been since she'd had any.

Not with Captain Sexypants right next door.

It was Luke's turn to stay awake all night staring at the ceiling, turning the dinner conversation over and over in his head. Claudia's disappointed face burned into his retinas. Her accusation taunted him on automatic replay.

I think you're the only one running around here.

He couldn't stay, for crying out loud. His career was at a crossroads. He was back to the point he had been a few years ago before his *wife* had screwed him over. He just needed to lure this one big client, to bring their multimillion-dollar account to the firm, then he'd be back on top again.

He was almost there.

People depended on him at work—both his clients and his team. He couldn't abandon them.

But could he really abandon Claudia now?

Again?

Sure, she had a team too, a very devoted team, but he couldn't bear the thought of her stuck in the resort-that-time-forgot where it was Groundhog Day twenty-four-seven. Not after the excitement—the anticipation—he'd witnessed today.

It was as if he'd taken her to the gates of paradise and opened them a crack so she could see inside…and then clanged them shut in her face.

Claudia would let their parents have their way. After all, she'd always loved the place just the way it was.

And she was a pleaser.

But would she still have that verve and bounce she was renowned for as each year went by and the if-onlys set in? If-onlys could cripple a person—he knew that better than most. If only he hadn't been so trusting of Philippa. If only he'd been paying more attention to the signs. If only he'd followed his own advice about the stupidity of office relationships.

If only he hadn't been such a fool…

If-onlys could eat you up inside. They could make you bitter; they could make you hard; they could wear you down.

He hated even the thought of that picture—Claudia with all the fizz and bubble gone. No more bounce. Lines around her eyes. A strained smile.

Hanging onto that damn clipboard of hers for dear life because if she didn't she might just smash it over the nearest hapless tourist's head.

He wouldn't wish if-onlys on his worst enemy.

Goddamn it.

He rolled over and punched his pillow hard. He was responsible for building up Claudia's expectations. He couldn't walk away from it now.

He was going to *have* to stay.

CHAPTER SEVEN

AFTER A NIGHT of tossing and turning and with his decision made, it was Luke's turn to barge in on Claudia. He'd heard the pipes in her shower going earlier so he knew she was up and about.

He knocked briefly on the interconnecting door then entered the room.

Except, she wasn't up and about.

The room was lit only by a slice of sunlight peeking through curtains ruffled by a stiff ocean breeze, but it was enough to see she was very much in bed. Very much asleep. And, he froze on the spot...

Very, very much naked.

For long moments he didn't know what to do—too shocked for any rationality as his brain tried to compute what he was seeing and his body waged a war with his conscience.

What are you doing, jerk? Get the hell out of here.

But...

She'll kill you if she wakes up and finds you staring at her like you've never seen a naked woman before.

But...

You are acting like a dirty perv. Stop it now!

And Luke knew it was true but he just didn't seem to be able to drag his eyes off Claudia's nakedness. He'd spent twenty-plus years of his life not thinking about her *like that* at all and within the space of a week he'd subjected her to a sleepy grope, was having erotic dreams about her and now he was perving at her in the buff.

He really needed to get the hell out.

But he couldn't move. Her breasts drew his gaze like

some horny fifteen-year-old boy at a peep show. She had both arms up over her head, one resting across her face, which drew her breasts up very nicely indeed. And there they sat, small, yes, but pleasingly pert with that enticing side-swell he'd felt in his hand a few days ago.

His palm tingled again in Pavlovian response.

Caramel-coloured areolas and nipples crowned the tips majestically and he swallowed as his blood sugar plummeted suddenly, his body craving a sugar hit.

A caramel hit.

Frightened by the urge to indulge, he fisted his palms as he dragged his gaze down. Her bare skin was pale and he absently wondered how she'd accomplished *that* living on top of a beach from the age of six. She'd told him she didn't have time for swimming but he hadn't thought she was serious.

Her waist was slender, boasting an equally petite belly button that sat out like a little pearl, just begging to be licked. Sucked.

He swallowed again.

Her hips flared into a gentle curve before the sheet hid the really interesting parts from his view. Although one leg was hidden in a tangle of fabric it managed to drag on the sheet enough to expose most of the other leg. His gaze wandered over her pink toenails, her delicate calf and one well-defined knee then all the way up to where the sheet stopped just shy of her groin.

He expelled a shaky breath. Claudia Davis was one sexy little package.

How the hell had he missed that?

A gust of wind blew the curtain, billowing it out, and the door creaked loudly behind him, dragging him out of his inertia.

Leave, leave now!

He turned to go. But another strong gust snatched the handle away just as he reached for it and the door slammed. Loud enough to wake the dead.

Sure as hell loud enough to wake the naked woman he'd been ogling.

He glanced over his shoulder as she sat bolt upright in bed and Luke's heart slammed as well. Louder than the door. Louder than the clanging chimes of doom that were ringing madly in his head.

Claudia woke with a start, her heart thundering in her chest, her startled gaze flying to the windows, momentarily confused. Was it another cyclone or was she still caught in the nightmare from the last one? The noise didn't come again and her pulse settled, her wild, dilated eyes constricting down to a more useful size. She looked around, her vision clearing to reveal a Luke of a different variety in her room.

He was standing still with his back to the bed. She frowned. 'Luke?'

He held his arms up as if in surrender but didn't turn around. 'I'm sorry,' he said. 'I thought you were awake. I didn't realise you were...'

Claudia frowned again. 'Asleep?' she clarified when it didn't appear as if he was going to finish his sentence.

He seemed to hesitate before saying, 'Er...yes...'

Claudia shrugged. 'Well, I'm awake now...kind of.'

Luke doubted it. He'd know the second she woke up fully.

Claudia yawned as she ran a hand through her hair. 'You might as well stay and talk to—'

Luke didn't have to wait much longer. The muscles in his shoulders tensed.

'Oh...my...*God*!'

Yep. *Now, she was awake.*

Claudia looked down at herself in horror. She was *naked*? She covered her breasts with an arm as she made a wild grab for the sheet, the quick impulsive tumble into bed the night before coming back in all its stupid glory.

She glared at Luke's back, the full implications sinking in pretty damn quick as she dragged the sheet right up to her chin and scuttled back until she was sitting ramrod straight against the bed head.

He'd seen her like this.

'How much did you see?' she demanded.

Luke, relieved to hear the rustle of the sheets, dropped his hands. 'I...' He was caught between lying to make her feel better and blurting out the truth.

Too bloody much.

He was never going to see her as that skinny six-year-old any more.

'Oh, God,' Claudia wailed, his silence more damning than any words. 'Please tell me I had the sheet on.'

'You did.'

He turned to assure her he hadn't seen *everything* but her frantic, 'Don't you dare turn around,' had him swivelling back to face the connecting door again.

Claudia clutched the sheets harder. 'What did you see?'

'Claude...'

Claudia wasn't in any mood to be placated. 'What. Did. You. See?'

'Just a...little bit of your...upper...part.' Luke waited for the lightning bolt to strike him dead.

Claudia shut her eyes. *Oh, dear God.* He'd seen her breasts. Within a handful of days he'd not only touched them but he'd seen them as well.

Damn, damn, damn.

'I'm really sorry...' Luke continued. 'I thought you were up...I thought I heard your shower pipes. I *did* knock.'

'How long were you standing there for?' she demanded.

Again Luke wasn't sure what the right answer was—the truth sure as hell wasn't pretty. 'Not...long...'

His hesitancy did not fill Claudia with confidence. 'Oh, God...you were, weren't you? Just standing there staring at me—*naked*—while I was asleep.'

'I...' He went to turn again.

Claudia pulled the sheet closer. 'Stop right there!'

Luke stopped mid-turn. 'This is ridiculous, Claude.'

Why was he facing the door when she'd obviously covered herself? He wanted to be able to plead his case and he needed to look at her for that. He needed her to know that he hadn't snuck into her room purely to perve on her.

Even if he had, in reality, not been able to tear his eyes off her.

But it hadn't been premeditated.

'I'm turning around,' he announced.

'No, you're not,' Claudia squeaked.

'Yes,' he said grimly. 'I am.' And did just that.

'Luke!' she gasped, outraged.

'Oh, relax,' he chided. Claudia had the sheet hiked up to her chin. 'You're more dressed than you were five minutes ago.'

Claudia blinked. 'Oh, nice, real nice, Luke,' she said scathingly.

Luke took a deep breath. 'I'm sorry,' he muttered, holding up his hands in a sign of contrition. 'But you're perfectly decent and I promise I'm not going to leap across the space between us and rip the sheet away so just ease up on it a little or the bloody thing will tear in two and then we'll be back at square one.'

'Yes.' Claudia nodded vigorously. 'With you gawking at me,' she said caustically, but she eased off, lowering the sheet to just below her chin.

Luke glared at her. 'I didn't...I wasn't...' He stopped because he *did* and he *was.* But it wasn't how she made it sound. Her eyebrow kicked up at his hesitancy and he shoved a hand through his hair in frustration.

Like with the grope incident, he was once again on the back foot. And like with the grope incident the best way to settle things was head-on.

'I came in to talk to you. I thought you were up and about. When I realised you were asleep, realised you were...naked I was *temporarily* rendered incapable of movement. I was... surprised.'

In shock was probably a better word. She'd told him just the other day when she'd been so scandalised by his own nudity, that she didn't sleep in the buff. It was a safe bet to assume that even if he had caught her in bed, that she'd at least be fully clothed and not *completely starkers.*

'I may have…probably…looked longer than I should have…' *Way longer.* 'I apologise. It wasn't my intention to…'

'Gawk? Perve? Ogle?'

Luke nodded. 'Yes. To all three.'

Claudia had to admit it was a fairly comprehensive apology but she wasn't sure she was ever going to be able to look at him again and not be aware of the fact that he'd seen her naked. She almost wanted to demand that he strip just so she could even the score.

More heat crept into her face at the thought—*how would that solve anything?* Didn't that make her just as pervy?

And what about those moments after she'd woken the other day to his hand on her breast and his erection snuggled against her? Hadn't she pushed back a little? Hadn't she stayed where she was instead of moving away? Hadn't she lain there wondering how good it might be if he slipped his hand under her shirt?

Could she claim to be so innocent where a sleeping Luke had been concerned?

The situation was too much and Claudia rested her forehead on her knees, feeling decidedly conflicted. How had they found themselves here?

'I really am sorry, Claude. What if I promise to permanently delete what I saw here today from my memory cells?'

Claudia blinked at the ludicrous offer—as if that were going to be possible. And then suddenly disbelief turned to affront. Wait. *Was that possible? Could he do it?* Did her assets leave that little an impression? She knew they were small but they were quite perky even if she did say so herself *and* in a push-up bra they looked even better.

Despite her embarrassment she felt more than a little miffed.

'Just like that?' she asked waspishly. 'My breasts are really that forgettable?' It was completely irrational to feel as if her femininity had been insulted.

She was supposed to still be mortified!

Luke frowned, trying to keep up with the sudden about-face. *What the—?* She was pissed at him now because he was offering to do the gentlemanly thing? Or was it just some trick question? Did she want him to remember it? Because frankly he didn't think there was enough will in the world to erase the memory of those delectable caramel nipples.

He was pretty sure they were going to feature in many future fantasy scenarios.

'No.' He shook his head 'God, no. Absolutely not.'

'Damn straight,' she muttered.

Luke frowned again. 'So...you don't want me to forget them?'

Claudia glared at him for rationalising something that had no rational basis. 'Yes, I do. Just maybe don't look as if it's so damn easy,' she grouched.

Luke knew this could be funny if it weren't so confusing. How could she sit there with the sheet pulled up to her neck like some Victorian virgin and look cranky and embarrassed and accusing all at once? As if her being naked were his fault?

He didn't think any man with a recent dose of jet lag should have to figure out the workings of the female brain.

'Oh, God,' he begged, rubbing his temples. 'I'm too tired and suspect I may have a Y chromosome too many for this conversation. Can we please just start again?'

Claudia noticed the cornered-male look on Luke's face and the absurdity of the situation hit her. If she weren't buck naked under the sheet, she might even have laughed. She felt the tension ease from her shoulders even if the heat in her cheeks didn't.

'Fine,' she huffed as her shoulders sagged and her lungs deflated. 'I'm sorry...I'm just...this isn't really in my playbook, you know?'

Hell, yeh, he knew. Walking in on a naked woman he could handle. Walking in on a naked Claudia—not so much. 'Well, if it's any consolation, it's not in mine either.'

Claudia smiled despite herself. 'Maybe this could be another of those things that we never speak of again?' she suggested.

Luke nodded vigorously. 'I think that's a very good idea.'

'Also, how about we both agree to knock and *wait* for an answer in future?'

'Deal.' Normally he would have held out his hand for a shake but he doubted she'd remove her grip from the sheets for anything. 'So I'm just going to go and pretend like this never happened.'

Claudia gave him a rueful smile. 'Sounds like a plan.'

It wasn't until he was halfway through the door that Claudia realised she still didn't know why he'd come to her room in the first place. 'Wait. What did you want to talk to me about?'

Luke turned at the unexpected question. With everything that had happened, he'd forgotten all about why he'd come to see Claudia in the first place. 'I'm going to stay. Help you manage the resort. At least until the spa is up and running anyway.'

Claudia stared at him for a moment, her heart beating almost as hard as it had when the door had slammed and scared the bejesus out of her. 'Really?'

Luke grinned. 'Really. Get dressed. I'll meet you downstairs. There are things to plan.'

Claudia didn't know what to say. Or do. If she hadn't been naked and just made a complete idiot of herself she'd have leapt out of bed and hugged him. As she'd hugged him hundreds of times in the past.

Instead she said and did nothing, just watched him disappear and the door shut after him.

Then she sank down onto her back and, grinning like a loon, pulled the sheet over her head and threw herself into a full naked body shimmy, squiggling her shoulders, arching her back off the bed and drumming her heels on the mattress.

She was getting her spa!

CHAPTER EIGHT

CLAUDIA'S HEAD WAS buzzing by the time she'd had a quick shower, thrown on her uniform and hightailed it downstairs. Not even the embarrassing thought of what had transpired in her room was enough to stop her from seeking Luke out. She found him breakfasting with everyone else.

'There you are, darling,' her mother said. 'Luke's just been telling us what you two have been up to.'

Claudia paused mid-sit, startled at the announcement as everyone beamed at her. Luke, sitting in the seat beside hers, gave her a wink.

'Has he now?' she murmured.

She knew he wouldn't have said anything about the…incident, but her mind couldn't help but go there. Especially as Luke was clearly amused at her mother's choice of words. His warm brown gaze was level with her breasts and she sat quickly to quell the memory as her nipples firmed against the fabric of her bra.

'It's wonderful,' Avery agreed, the excitement in her voice sharpening her accent.

'Yes,' his mother agreed. 'You are sure your firm will understand, though?' Gloria pressed.

Luke gave a short nod because he knew his decision to work remotely would not be popular with the partners. Major adjustments would have to be made to accommodate it. Not to mention he'd be working two demanding jobs. Long days at the resort would be backed up by long hours into the night when clients were awake on the other side of the world.

He couldn't see himself getting much sleep.

But these were extenuating circumstances and at least these days they had the technology to run with something like this so, why not? The Internet made distance a non-sense—email, iClouds, Skype, teleconferencing—anything was possible.

'It'll take some setting up,' he dismissed, 'but it shouldn't be a problem.'

'There now,' Avery said to two sets of parents. 'You can get back to your holiday.'

Claudia wanted to kiss her. 'That's right,' she agreed quickly. 'You guys retired so other people could wait on you for a change. You really don't have to worry about the Tropicana.'

Her mother beamed. 'Excellent. I feel so much better knowing the two of you will be doing this together.'

There was general conversation over breakfast about the new addition but Claudia felt inadequately prepared to answer a lot of the questions raised. 'To be honest,' she admitted, 'I've never been to a spa and I think I've only ever had one massage in my entire life.' She looked at Avery, who was more accustomed to the day-spa life. 'That time in Bali... on the beach...do you remember?'

'Oh, yes.' Avery smiled. 'Your masseuse was an ancient woman with hardly any teeth.'

Claudia nodded. 'And yours was that buff young guy wearing a shirt that showed off every perfect muscle in his abs.'

Avery's smile turned dreamy. 'Oh, yes,' she sighed. '*Incredible* fingers too.'

Jonah looked unimpressed. 'I hate him already,' he murmured, gliding a possessive hand onto Avery's shoulder, and Claudia felt a pang hit her square in the chest at Jonah's caveman display. She glanced quickly at Luke, then glanced away again.

Avery smiled at Jonah and the look they shared took the pang into chest-pain territory. 'We'll have to do some tours,'

Avery said enthusiastically as she dragged her gaze away from Jonah. 'See what's out there. See what's new and innovative and popular.'

'That will be impossible for a while,' Claudia dismissed. 'We have one hundred rooms upstairs that all need to be assessed one by one and given a good clean so we can at least offer them to the public and have some income again.'

All their efforts last week had been concentrated on the outside clean-up. Apart from a cursory examination of the rooms that had been thankfully largely untouched, they hadn't worried about them at all. But they were going to need to be electrically checked at the very least.

'We'll have to discount them,' Luke said. 'This place isn't exactly paradise any more.'

Claudia nodded automatically at Luke's shrewd business assessment, ignoring her emotional response to his words. If she thought too hard about their paradise lost it would break her heart, and they needed to be practical.

'And before anyone comes we'll have to put in all new landscaping,' she said. 'The resort may be a long way off its established old self but I'd like to make a good impression when we welcome back our first guests.'

'We can pitch in and help you with that stuff,' Lena said.

'Harry and I can help with the landscaping,' Brian said.

'And your mother and I can contact all cancelled and future guests and see who might still be interested in a basic cheapy holiday,' Gloria confirmed.

Lena nodded. 'We're here, we might as well put ourselves to good use, if you'll have us. And then when the guests start to arrive we can push off again and let you kids get on with it.'

'Of course we'll have you,' Claudia said reassuringly. 'This is your place—you don't need to ask permission to stay. There will always be rooms here for you.'

'Good to know,' Brian said gruffly. 'But we've got at least a year left on our trip so don't keep them blocked for us.'

'You'll come back for the opening of the spa, though?' Claudia insisted.

Brian patted her hand. 'Try keeping us away, love.'

Claudia smiled at Luke's father—she'd always had a soft spot for him. 'Thank you.'

'So it could be a while before we get to check out spas,' Avery said wistfully.

'Not necessarily,' Jonah said. 'The best time to go will be before the paying customers come back. You and Claude might be able to squeeze something in.'

'Cairns is the best place,' Isis added.

Claudia doubted they'd have time to scratch but she nodded anyway. 'We'll see how we're tracking.'

An hour later Luke had made a list of things he was going to need to set up a makeshift office in the Mai Tai. Jonah was taking the chopper into Cairns for business and had offered him a ride. He was coming down the stairs as Claudia was heading up, her clipboard clutched to her chest.

They slowed as they neared, her on the step below him. 'I'm off to Cairns with Jonah for a quick trip. Anything you need?' he asked, waving his list in front of her.

Claudia shook her head as she looked up at him. *Way* up. 'Thanks. I've given him a list already.'

Luke nodded. 'You off to assess the rooms?' he asked

'Yes. I'm tackling the suites. Isis is doing the first floor. Avery the second.'

'And the ground-floor rooms?'

'I'll do them after I've done the suites.'

Claudia shifted her feet nervously. Her gaze was level with his chest, the T-shirt he was wearing gracing its lean musculature like a velvet glove. She remembered how hard that chest had felt behind her the other day. Then she remembered what had happened *today*.

It was hard to believe on this grand staircase in this voluminous foyer that she could suddenly feel claustrophobic.

She looked down at her clipboard, confused by the skip in her pulse. She dropped it slightly away from her body, relieved to have something else to look at even if it was just pages and pages of pristine maintenance reports awaiting her neat handwriting.

'We're just taking notes today,' she said for something to say in case his head was where her head was at. 'Don, he's a local electrician, is coming in two days for the electrical checks. He's crazy busy but we did him a good deal on his daughter's wedding here a few years back so he's squeezing us in.'

'Yay for Don.' Luke smiled. The clipboard movement had pulled down her blouse slightly revealing her usually well-covered décolletage. From his vantage point he could see some swell rising out of a soft-looking emerald-green fabric edged with black ribbon.

Was that satin?

It *looked* like satin, soft and shiny.

And then he was thinking about her breasts again. When, true to his word, he *had* been trying hard not to.

Crap.

Who knew Claudia favoured sexy lingerie beneath her awful uniform? He'd never look at her polyester blouse the same again.

Claudia took a step to the side so she could walk around him, then hesitated for a moment. Her eyes glued to the clipboard, she murmured, 'I haven't really said thank you.'

Luke shrugged. 'It's okay. I owe you for being such a stubborn bastard last year. I should have done what I'm doing now back then. It's just that things at work were…'

Luke didn't really want to get into it but he'd still been under the gun from losing the account his wife—*ex-wife*—had stolen from him. It was the main reason he'd wanted the resort handed over to a big chain—his career was in crisis and the resort had been an unwanted distraction.

'Were?' she prompted softly.

Luke grimaced at the familiar bitter taste the memory left in his mouth. A flash of black ribbon caught his eye again and yanked him out of the past. 'It doesn't matter. The point is I'm here now and I'm in.'

'And I'm very, very thankful.' Claudia smiled. 'We'll have to remember this day and celebrate it next year as the day we really put our mark on the Tropicana.'

Luke smiled back before the full import of her words sank in. His smile slowly faded. 'You do know this is only temporary, Claude? I did say just until the spa was up and running. I'm not staying for good. I'll be heading back to the UK as soon as things are settled here. You're more than capable of managing the place solo.'

Solo. Claudia swallowed. Why did that word sound so bloody lonely?

'Yes...of course,' she said with a dismissive shake of her head. 'Of course.'

Even though she felt like a complete idiot. He'd said this morning it was just until the spa was open but she'd been off building castles in the sky. Spinning fantasies of them running the resort together for the next twenty years as their parents had done.

Luke wasn't sure about the overly bright light in her eyes. The last thing he wanted to do was to get her hopes up. 'My life is there, Claude,' he murmured.

Claudia forced a smile onto her face, determined not to show him how much those five words hurt, no matter how gently he'd said them.

My life is there, Claude.

His life was there. Hers was here. She'd do well to remember that over the coming months.

'Of course,' she assured him, her voice more definitive this time. 'I know. And you're right, I'm perfectly capable of managing the Tropicana.'

Luke nodded, satisfied. 'No one better.' He grinned as soft green satin taunted his peripheral vision.

Claudia grinned back even though it felt as if it had been slashed into her face with a carving knife. 'Well,' she said as she put her foot on the next step, pulling the clipboard back to her chest. 'Guess I'd better get on. I'll see you when you get back from Cairns.'

Luke nodded, disgusted in his disappointment that the cleavage show was over. 'Yep. Should be back in a couple of hours.'

'Okay,' she said.

Visions of green satin, black ribbon and caramel nipples taunted him as he continued down the stairs.

CHAPTER NINE

Two weeks flew by. Two weeks of getting rooms and grounds ready to open again. All the rooms had escaped major damage. Some power points had blown and three rooms had sustained some minor water damage to the carpet when their windows, despite the cyclone taping, had cracked under the force of the wind and allowed water to trickle in.

But three out of one hundred was good going, considering the other accommodation blocks on the property had been completely smashed.

The landscaping was a big job hampered by transport difficulties due to the state of the roads. The extensive Tropicana gardens that had taken forty years to establish and made guests feel as if they were living in a tropical paradise had been about fifty per cent destroyed in a matter of a few hours.

They would take many years to get back to the way they were but thankfully some of the older trees and vegetation had been left intact so they didn't have to start from scratch.

The problem was supply of raw material. Mature plants and trees and things like mulch were in high demand post-cyclone and difficult to source, which meant the landscaping would be an ongoing job. But they managed with what they could get, transforming the grounds from decimated to rejuvenated in an amazingly short time.

Gloria and Lena worked the phones like the true veteran hotel professionals they were. Claudia was thankful that they'd stayed on to lend a hand, knowing the process would have been much longer without them and it also freed her up to help Isis and Avery get everything shipshape on the inside.

Next week they were welcoming their first trickle of guests—fifteen rooms booked. And the week after that they had a further twenty. Claudia had set a target of fifty per cent occupancy by the time the spa opened a few months down the track and hoped to be back at full occupancy for the summer season at the end of the year.

It was March—it was doable.

They were never going to have the numbers they had before simply because the accommodation units that had been scattered throughout the property had been flattened and were not going to be replaced.

The hope was that the higher-end customers would make up the shortfall.

Claudia and Luke set a couple of hours aside each afternoon to work on plans for the spa. They'd contacted a local builder who Claudia trusted to do the job and consulted a local architect. They just needed to get plans drawn up and then council approvals and other such legalities under way.

They kept things businesslike between them, barely talking outside what was needed for the Tropicana and rarely seeing each other outside anything to do with the plans. Unlike their childhood, the interconnecting door was *not* chocked open and they *never* entered each other's rooms without knocking and receiving clear direction to do so!

It was a grope-free, nudity-free zone.

And things could have been awkward between them had they not been so busy. But everyone was busy, everyone had their heads down, so it was easy for them to just follow suit and pretend there wasn't time for chit-chat.

Luke was probably busiest of all working two jobs. After a back-breaking day out landscaping, he was up late into the night working on UK time in the world of advertising. He rarely got into bed before two a.m. And if he was tired, well, he knew there was a queue he could join. Everyone was working hard. Everyone was tired.

On Friday morning at breakfast, Avery slipped a sheaf of papers across the table to Claudia. 'I spent a few hours on the net last night and I think we should check out these three day-spas in Cairns.' She looked at Luke. 'You too. Seeing them firsthand is much better than getting second-hand descriptions.'

'Yep. Count me in,' he said.

Claudia flicked through the printed pages. 'These look good.' She handed them to Luke.

'I can make a booking for us to have something different at each one for tomorrow?' Avery said.

'Tomorrow?' Claudia worried her bottom lip. 'Do you think we should be tripping off for mani-pedis with the first guests arriving on Monday?'

'It's the perfect time,' Gloria encouraged. 'There's nothing much to do between now and then and you won't get a chance after Monday.'

Claudia nodded. 'I suppose.'

'Jonah can take us all in the chopper, make a bit of a day of it,' Avery suggested.

'You kids have worked really hard,' Brian said. 'Why don't you make a night of it? Get away from here for twenty-four hours and relax? Stay in a swanky hotel, be waited on. You're going to be the ones doing all the waiting soon.'

'Oh, yes,' Avery said, clearly warming to the subject. 'We could go dancing,' she said, turning to Jonah, gliding her hand onto his forearm. 'It's been ages since we danced.'

Jonah smiled and kissed the tip of Avery's nose. 'Yes, it has.'

Avery squeezed his arm. 'Claude, what's the name of the hotel where Raoul hangs out? That has that Latin dancing on Saturday night?'

Luke frowned. Raoul? Why was that name familiar?

'The Quay,' Claudia said, wondering how a trip to a day spa had suddenly become twenty-four hours of debauchery complete with Latin dancing.

'Yes, that's it,' Avery exclaimed. 'Oh, let's do that,' she enthused, looking first at Claudia and then at Jonah.

Luke looked at Claudia. He didn't want to dance with her. Getting that close after what had transpired between them didn't seem like such a good idea. He turned to Jonah. 'No,' he said to his friend. 'I have to work tomorrow night.'

'It's Saturday.'

'My job's twenty-four-seven.'

'Good thing you're so attached to your phone, then,' Jonah said mildly.

Luke shot his friend a measured stare. 'I don't dance.'

Jonah grinned at Luke. 'So don't.' Then he smiled down at Avery. 'Your wish is my command,' he said.

'Oh, I'm not sure—' Claudia started.

'Oh, go on, darling,' her mother quickly interrupted. 'It's a brilliant idea. You guys have been working yourselves into the ground. Go and let your hair down for a night.'

'Right, that's settled, then,' Avery announced as she scraped her chair back and stood. 'I'm going to go book us in at the spas and then the hotel.'

She looked directly at Claudia and Luke, who were sitting next to each other in the seats that had somehow, by silent majority, been relegated to them. 'Do you guys want separate rooms or are you okay with twin share?' she asked.

'Separate,' they both said in unison.

Avery shot them a mischievous grin before she practically skipped out of the room, and Claudia narrowed her eyes.

'Guess we're going dancing.' Jonah grinned as he watched Avery go.

A flash of green satin trimmed with black ribbon floated through Luke's mind. There was no way he was getting on that dance floor.

* * *

'So what are you wearing out dancing?' Avery asked Claudia later that evening as she sat on Claudia's bed almost at the bottom of her second glass of wine and watching a movie on cable TV. It had become a regular thing for them ever since Avery had come to work at the Tropicana over a year ago—Friday night was girlfriend night.

It was something that Claudia always looked forward to and appreciated that Avery still tore herself away from the lovely Jonah to spend some quality time with her bestie. But tonight, Claudia wished Avery had let Jonah talk her into staying home.

'Hadn't thought about it,' Claudia dismissed, hoping her voice sounded light and disinterested and didn't betray the mass of nerves screwing her stomach into a tight ball.

Avery frowned at her. 'What? I don't believe it. You love to dance.'

Sure, she loved to dance. That was how she'd got involved with Raoul. Raoul ran the dance lessons at the Tropicana and had been her occasional lover for the last five years. But she didn't want to sit all night and watch Luke dance with other women either. 'Guess I'm just not in the mood,' she said.

'Oh, come on,' Avery teased. 'Raoul could be there. How long has it been since you guys hooked up?'

Claudia didn't have to think about it—she knew exactly. 'Since just before the resort got handed to me.'

Avery sat up, nearly spilling some of her wine. 'That was nearly eighteen months ago.' She sounded horrified.

'So?'

Avery gaped at her nonchalant reply. 'That's an awful long time to go without some lovin', Claude.'

Claudia gave an exasperated sigh. 'I know you're all loved up,' she said, her tone as dry as powdery sand under a hot midday sun, 'but, trust me, you don't die from lack of sex, Avery.'

'Yeah, but...what's the point of living?'

Claudia laughed then, she couldn't help herself. Avery's expression was priceless. 'I've been a little busy,' she finally said.

Avery waggled her finger in front of her friend's face. 'All work and no play makes Claude a dull girl.' She placed her wine glass down on the bedside table and slipped off the bed. 'Let's see what's in your cupboard that might get Raoul's pulse racing.'

Claudia watched her go, her enthusiasm for that idea utterly underwhelming. 'I'm not going to *hook up* with Raoul in front of Luke,' she grouched as Avery pulled open the cupboard doors.

Avery turned, a frown marring her forehead. 'Why not?'

Claudia squirmed a little. The reason sounded stupid in her head—she could only imagine how dumb it was going to sound out loud.

'Claude?' Avery prompted.

Claudia knew that tone in her friend's voice all too well. 'It'll be too…weird with Raoul…in front of Luke.'

Avery blinked. 'Why?'

Claudia shook her head—she wished she knew. 'I don't know. It just would be.'

A sudden speculative spark flared to life in Avery's shrewd eyes and she forgot the wardrobe as she returned to the bed and sat on the edge with one leg tucked up under her, the other firmly on the ground.

'Is there something going on with you and Captain Sexypants?' she asked.

Claudia almost laughed out loud, both at the nickname that seemed to have stuck and the preposterous suggestion. Something going on with her and Luke?

Impossible.

Even if he did know what she looked like naked *and* what her breast felt like. 'No,' she said.

Avery dropped her head slightly to the side as if she was trying to see deep into Claudia's heart. 'I think there's stuff you're not telling me, Ms Claude.' She folded her arms. 'Spill.'

Claudia thought long and hard about keeping what had gone on between her and Luke to herself, but a part of her wanted to get it off her chest so badly, to analyse it to death in that secret girly-gossip way she used to enjoy with Avery, she could hardly bear it any more.

So she spilled. About the grope incident. About her walking in on him naked. About him walking in on her naked. And it felt so damn good to unburden it. It felt just like it used to do when they'd been teenagers, sharing all their angsty, hormone-ridden secrets.

'So you *do* have a thing for Captain Sexypants?' Avery, who had been remarkably quiet throughout, said.

'No,' Claudia denied, and when Avery gave her that *watch it, Pinocchio* look she just said, 'I can't. He's *Luke*. He's a friend I've known for ever. Our parents are *best friends*. He's divorced and bitter on love. *And* he lives on the opposite side of the world.'

Claudia shook her head at Avery's *what-else-have-you-got?* eyebrow-raise. 'He's *leaving,* Avery.'

Avery reached out and grabbed her friend's hand. 'So was I,' she said. 'But I didn't.' Then she sprang off the bed. 'It ain't over till the fat lady sings,' she said, sounding more American than ever. 'And besides, I don't think there's any harm in letting Captain Sexypants know *exactly* what it is he's leaving behind.'

Claudia watched her friend return to the wardrobe, pulling out dresses, wishing she had just an inch of Avery's confidence. 'I know just the one,' she said.

Resigned to her fate, Claudia watched. 'There's that royal blue one I wear to our voodoo nights,' she said.

'Oh, no, no, no,' Avery said, throwing dresses on the ground now. 'I know exactly the one. The red velvety one. It flutters around your ankles, fits you like a glove, has that halter neck and huge side split.'

Claudia blanched at the suggestion. 'I think that's a bit OTT, don't you?'

Avery's voice was muffled as she disappeared into the cupboard a little more but Claudia could still make out her friend's denial. 'Nope. Raoul goes a little crazy every time you wear that dress and that's exactly the effect you're after.' And then a few seconds later, she heard the proclamation, 'Aha!'

Avery walked out of the cupboard brandishing the dress in question. 'This one.'

Claudia shook her head. 'No.'

Avery ignored her. 'We're going dancing. *This* is your dancing dress.'

'It is?'

'It is now.' Avery grinned at her. 'Try it on.'

'Avery...' Claudia glared at her best friend. 'No.'

'You know I'm just going to harp on about it all night until you do, so you might as well get it over with now.'

Claudia sighed at the truth of it. Avery could be very persistent, particularly after two glasses of wine. 'Fine,' she huffed, climbing off the bed. 'Give it to me.'

Claudia took the dress from Avery and marched into the bathroom, quickly stripping off her uniform and throwing the dress over her head before marching back out again.

Avery beamed at her as she appeared. Then she reached over and pulled Claudia's hair out of her ponytail, fluffing it up a little.

She grinned. 'Well, hello, Kryptonite.'

CHAPTER TEN

THEY WERE AT the first day-spa venue at nine o'clock the following morning. Jonah had left them to spend the morning checking up on Charter North, his exceedingly successful charter business, which he'd been neglecting to help the Tropicana back on its feet. He had a good second in command so he wasn't worried, but he felt as if he should at least look in and check on progress. He was to join them again for lunch.

The first two spas were attached to hotels and the managers were happy to show them around. Avery and Claudia had a manicure and a pedicure at the first one while Luke sat at a table with his phone and his laptop. The second one they both indulged in facials and again Luke had the phone glued to his ear.

They caught up with Jonah at the marina for lunch. It was more of a business lunch with lots of constructive conversation about the pros and cons of what they'd seen so far and they were only interrupted once by Luke's phone.

'It'll be interesting to see what the next place is like by comparison,' Avery said as she sipped at an icy cold mineral water. 'It's a stand-alone and is *very* exclusive.'

'More the kind of thing we'll be doing,' Luke said.

'Yep.' Avery nodded. 'I've booked us all in for massages.'

Luke frowned. 'What? I don't want a massage.'

Claudia thought if anyone could do with a massage right now it was Luke. He'd been working all morning at his computer on some crisis or other that had cropped up overnight in London.

Avery shot him an exasperated look. '*You* need a massage more than all of us combined,' she said and Claudia hid a smile behind her napkin at Avery in bossy mode. 'You've been saving the world all morning on your damn phone, not to mention both you and Jonah have been doing some pretty hard physical labour these last couple of weeks. I'm sure there are some kinks that could do with some ironing out and I've booked it for you and you *will* have it and what's more you better bloody enjoy it.'

Luke glanced at Jonah, who also seemed to be having trouble keeping a smile off his face. He held up his hands in surrender. 'It's a massage, man. There are worse ways to spend an hour.'

Luke shook his head in disgust. 'You are so whipped.'

Jonah grinned back at him. 'That I am.'

Luke rolled his eyes. 'I guess I do have some kinks.'

Claudia almost spat her orange juice all over the table. Yeah, like groping and perving on sleeping women.

Avery beamed. 'Atta boy,' she said, reaching over and patting his arm. She flicked a quick glance at Claudia. 'Just think, you'll be all loose and limber for when you spin Claude around the dance floor tonight. Win-win.'

Luke sensed Claudia tense beside him. An echoing tension crept into his shoulders.

Looked like they both needed that massage.

When they arrived at the spa they checked in and were all given a tour of the facility. Then they were ushered into separate change rooms to undress and get into the robes provided in preparation for their massages. Jonah and Luke were shown the male change rooms. Luke's phone rang the second his shirt was off.

'You miss your massage and Avery is going to be very displeased,' Jonah said as Luke reached for it.

Luke looked at the London number on his screen. 'This won't take long,' he said. 'Go on without me.'

Jonah clapped Luke on the shoulder. 'You know she'll come in and get you if you take too long.'

'Two minutes,' Luke said as he pushed the answer button.

Ten minutes later, Luke stepped out of the change room, swathed in soft white towelling. Despite his earlier protest he was actually looking forward to it. He was hyper-aware of the tension in his neck that had cranked up during the phone call and his muscles *did* ache from all the physical activity he'd been doing.

He'd become unaccustomed to that kind of heavy labour. Sure, he worked out at the gym regularly and jogged along London streets in the early morning most days—he loved the pavements that ran alongside the Thames, even in winter— but he hadn't been this physically challenged in a long time.

An attractive brunette met him. 'Hi, I'm Sherry,' she said. 'I'll be doing your massage today.'

Luke nodded. 'Nice to meet you.'

She smiled at him and Luke got the impression she wasn't going to find his massage a chore in any way, shape or form. He smiled back. Jonah was right. There were worse ways to spend an hour.

'This way,' she said and gestured for him to follow her.

Sherry walked down a carpeted hallway with subdued lighting and opened a door to the right at the end of the corridor. She smiled at him again as she indicated he should precede her. A light floral aroma greeted him before he even entered and Luke noted the subdued lighting extended into the interior of the room as he put his foot over the threshold.

Then several things registered all at once. The presence of two tables, one empty, the other with a person—a female person. She was lying on her belly with nothing but a towel covering her butt and acres of bare, glistening skin exposed to his gaze. Candlelight glowed in the oil covering her body and a man worked said oil into the backs of her legs.

Claudia?

And then while his brain desperately tried to compute the

images in those first few surprising seconds he heard, 'Oh, dear Lord in heaven, that's *soooo goooood.*'

Actually it was more a groan. She'd definitely groaned it. *Claudia* had groaned it.

He watched the male masseur's hands slide all the way up from the back of Claudia's knee to the top of her thigh—a little too close to where it joined her butt for Luke's liking.

'What the hell?'

Even in Droolsville, the low growl yanked Claudia out of her bliss. She gasped as she half raised her chest off the table and then remembered she was wearing only a towel that wasn't currently covering much of her at all.

Caught in flagrante again!

She lowered herself, looking over her shoulder at Luke looking better than any man had a right to in a white fluffy gown.

'What are you doing in here?' she snapped, heat in her cheeks—was she destined to suffer from a terminal lack of clothing around him?

'What am *I* doing in here? This is where I was brought. What are *you* doing in here?'

'Oh, I'm sorry,' Sherry said, looking as confused as the rest of them. 'I think there's been a terrible mistake. I thought this was a couple's massage? Like the other two? I thought the other woman said…I thought you were…together.'

Luke glared at the guy whose hands had stilled on the back of Claudia's thigh. The masseur removed them, eyeing Luke warily. 'No,' Luke said tersely. 'We're not.'

'Oh, dear, I'm terribly, terribly sorry,' Sherry apologised, wringing her hands, looking more mortified than Luke had ever seen another living person. 'No worries,' she said, 'I can rebook you. It'll need to be tomorrow—we're fully booked today.'

'I won't be here tomorrow.'

'Perhaps another day,' Sherry the mortified asked.

Luke's jaw clenched. 'I don't need a massage,' he said and turned to go.

Claudia frowned as a wave of crankiness accompanied Luke's dismissive statement. Oh, no. Avery was right—he *did* need a massage. Now more than ever—*clearly*! And she'd be damned if she was going to be the one to stand in the way of it.

'Wait,' she said as he neared the door. 'You stay and I'll go. You're working two jobs and long hours. You need the massage more than I do.'

Luke stopped and turned to face her. 'I'm fine, Claude.'

'No,' she said. 'I insist.' She craned her neck around further until she could see the man whose fingers had been working magic until this rather abrupt interruption.

'Can you cover me please, Marco?'

Marco went to shift the towel from Claudia's derrière and Luke stepped forward on an alarmed, 'No.' Marco stopped and shot Luke a puzzled look. Claudia was looking at him as if he'd lost his mind as well. But he'd seen more than enough of her skin for one day.

In the few weeks he'd been home he'd seen more than enough of Claudia to last him a lifetime.

'You've had more stress than all of us combined,' he said. 'And besides…' Luke glanced at Marco. 'You *sounded* like you were enjoying it. Very much.'

Claudia couldn't deny how much she'd been enjoying it. How much she'd been looking forward to a massage ever since Avery had mentioned the spa idea yesterday. And to deny herself Marco's fingers would be a particularly heinous form of torture.

'Oh, for God's sake,' she said, suddenly annoyed at him and herself for acting as if they were in some Victorian melodrama. It wasn't as if they hadn't already seen each other in next to nothing. 'The table's here, Sherry is here…we shared a bed for years. Just lie down already.'

Luke was aware of the two masseurs exchanging looks.

'We were kids,' he clarified to Sherry. And then flicked his gaze back to Claudia. 'I'm fine.'

Claudia glared at him. 'And dandy?' And then when he didn't look as if he was going to give in she said, 'You're making me tense just looking at you.'

Which really wasn't a lie. The thought of what he had on under that robe was making her really freaking tense. They'd asked her to strip everything off so she assumed he had too...

Luke held Claudia's gaze for long seconds. 'Fine,' he muttered again. He turned to Sherry. 'Where do you want me?'

Claudia wasn't sure if he was being deliberately provocative but she gritted her teeth as she placed her face back in the hole on the massage table and prepared to go back to her happy place.

Not easy to do with six feet four inches of pissed-off man right beside her.

Naked pissed-off man.

Luke found it difficult to relax even under Sherry's expert hands. Everything in the environment around him was conducive to a state of relaxation—the low lighting, the essential oils, the rainforest music—he just couldn't find it. All he could see behind his shut lids was big male hands on the backs of Claudia's legs, slippery and kneading.

And they *weren't* Marco's.

Luke tensed even more as the deep melodic timbre of Marco's voice reached him. 'I'll lift the towel if you want to turn over to your front.' Claudia's table creaked slightly and he swallowed as he tried not to think about her turning over.

Do not think about Claudia naked and jiggling.

'You're very tense,' Sherry murmured somewhere near his ear in the same melodic timbre that blended with the music and ambience.

He was pretty sure he heard Claudia snort. 'My boss has had me working like a lackey these last two weeks,' he murmured.

Another snort from Claudia's direction.

Luke smiled to himself as silence descended upon the room again. He wondered what the hell Sherry and Marco thought of *this* particular couple's massage. He could just picture them raising their eyebrows at each other and shrugging their shoulders. They were undoubtedly more used to couples holding hands and bringing their own CDs of Gregorian chants than a couple who could barely say a civil word to each other.

Claudia was grateful for the warm cloth that Marco placed over her eyes. She'd copped an eyeful of Luke's broad smooth back as she'd turned. Sherry's hands glided all over the expanse of him, and she was alternately turned on and jealous.

She could massage the hell out of that back. She'd been told she gave a mean back rub and Luke's muscles looked as if they were made to be kneaded.

Her heart crashed around in her chest as unhelpful images sprang to mind. No matter how hard she tried to let the drugging massage take her away, to concentrate on the long smooth strokes from expert hands, the image of *her* hands on Luke's back—and his legs, and his chest—kept her well and truly anchored to the room.

To the man lying less than two metres away.

'I'll hold the towel so you can flip over.'

Claudia tensed and held her breath as Sherry's command to Luke seemed loud in the room. What would he see when he turned over? Another man's hands massaging oil into her legs? Her bare shoulders and chest? The towel clinging precariously to nipples and just skimming her upper thighs? Her exposed legs?

A lot of skin. Oily and slippery as his had looked, the flicker of flame casting a warm glow over it, bathing it in golden light.

Would it remind him of *that* morning?

Would he even look?

'Just the back's fine,' Luke said.

Luke took a deep steady breath. The last thing he needed was to turn over. He'd spent twenty minutes trying not to think about the fact that a naked woman was having her body oiled and kneaded right beside him.

And not just *any* woman.

Claudia.

He'd tried really hard not to think about them being alone at the end of this, all slippery and oily and essentially naked. He closed his mind off to wondering how much weight one of these tables could bear. And he'd definitely not let himself go down the mental path of I-wonder-if-these-doors-have-locks.

He'd got this far without an erection but he knew he had a precarious control on his libido and he didn't trust himself to turn over and not glance Claudia's way one more time.

His libido didn't need that kind of trouble.

'Are you sure?' Sherry asked.

He'd never been surer of anything in his life. 'Positive.'

'Well, let me work a bit more on your neck,' she offered. 'I'm surprised it hasn't snapped right off your shoulders it's so taut.'

'Thank you,' he murmured.

Because his head *was* about ready to snap right off. And he was damned if he was going to leave this room before Claudia did. He was keeping his head down and his face firmly jammed in the cut-out until Claudia and her robe had departed.

CHAPTER ELEVEN

'AVERY SHAW, YOU switched the dresses.'

'Ah…yes. I can explain that.'

Claudia gripped the phone. 'Oh, really? How?'

'I had a hunch you'd chicken out on the red dress so I performed a little…switcheroo this morning.'

'You did what?' Claudia blustered into the mouthpiece. 'When?'

'Well, I enlisted—'

'Jonah,' Claudia said in disgust, the incident that had momentarily puzzled her this morning now making sense. She should have gone with her instincts when Jonah required her assistance to choose which font they were going to use on the new garden signs.

As if he gave a rat's arse about fonts.

'Don't blame him,' Avery pleaded down the line, jumping to Jonah's defence—as if the brawny, muscle-bound, lovesick fool needed it.

As if he gave a rat's arse about Claudia's displeasure. He was clearly too busy thinking about *his own* pleasure.

'I cajoled him into it,' Avery continued.

Claudia snorted. 'I bet it didn't take much.'

'He told me he didn't think I should interfere.'

Claudia wasn't swayed by Avery's standing-by-her-man act—even if it was the sweetest thing. 'He's a clever guy,' Claudia said dryly.

'I'm not interfering, Claude…not really…'

Claudia touched the crushed-velvet fabric laid out on her

hotel room bedspread and tried not to be seduced by its glamour. 'You booked us into a couple's massage!'

'I *did not* book you in as a couple,' Avery protested for the umpteenth time. 'I can't help it if Sherry got the impression you two were…together.'

'And then,' Claudia said, ignoring Avery's arguments because they both knew damn well who had planted those impressions in Sherry's head, 'you sabotage my wardrobe.'

'We're going dancing—you need your dancing dress.'

Claudia glanced at the dress again, then firmly turned her back on it. 'The blue one is fine.'

'Of course it's fine. But the red one…' Claudia heard Avery sigh loud and clear across the connection and rolled her eyes. 'The red one is *ooh-la-la*. Every man's head is going to turn when you walk into the room in that thing. Every man is going to want to dance with you. Your dance card will be full.'

'I don't want every man's head turning,' Claudia said waspishly. 'I don't want to dance with every man in the room.'

There was a pause for a moment before Avery's voice said softly in her ear, 'Just the one?'

'Avery,' she warned. 'Forget about Luke and I.'

There was another silence during which Claudia could almost hear the thoughts whizzing around in her friend's head.

'We can never have that kind of relationship, Avery,' Claudia said, gentler his time. 'We've known each other too long. Too well. And he's too cynical about love.'

It helped to say the words out loud, and not just for Avery's sake. 'It's never going to happen.'

A brief pause followed this time but Avery was never one to be kept down. 'So that's even more reason to go out and let your hair down,' she enthused. 'You deserve a night on the town. So go knock 'em all dead in that dress.'

Claudia turned back to face the dress. 'I don't know, Avery…I'm kind of tired.'

It was a lie, of course; the massage had rejuvenated her from the inside out and it had been such a long time since she'd danced...and if Luke wasn't going to be there she'd definitely be up for a party.

She stroked a finger down the deep V of the halter neck.

'Oh, come on, you know you'll have fun once you get into it.'

'I suppose...'

Avery tutted in her ear. 'Suppose? Phfft! You know you'll love it. Now, say it out loud. I, Claudia Davis, will put on my red dress and shake my booty all night and I *will* enjoy it.'

'Avery.'

'Say it!'

Claudia sighed and repeated the requested phrase. 'Louder,' Avery said. 'Say it with feeling.' Claudia said it louder. And with feeling.

'There, now, doesn't that feel better?' she asked.

Claudia smiled. 'Yeah, it does.'

'Good,' Avery chirped and the triumph in her voice was infectious. 'Now, what have you learned from this incident?' she asked, then gleefully supplied the answer to the rhetorical question. 'That Avery's always right.'

Claudia laughed. 'No. Try never trust someone who has access to your door key.'

Luke almost had a heart attack when he called on Claudia to pick her up right on the dot of seven as they'd prearranged. She was swathed head to ankle in slinky dark red velvet. Like crushed raspberries.

And he was starving.

Her hair was in some kind of messy up-do that trailed blonde wisps down her nape, her shoulders were bare, her *cleavage* was bare—*do not think about her breasts*—and she had on some strappy shoes with ten crimson toenails flashing at him in all their sinful glory.

She looked as if she'd been shrink-wrapped from chest

to hips into the dress before it flowed around her thighs and calves.

'You're wearing *that*?'

Claudia supposed she could have taken offence at his rather rude greeting, but she wasn't stupid and she didn't believe in acting obtuse around men. It was clear she'd stunned him and her feminine ego swelled dramatically.

'And good evening to you too,' she murmured, pulling her door closed.

Luke ignored the gentle reprimand. He looked into the depths of her cleavage. 'Don't you have some kind of…' he waved his hands in the general direction of her shoulders and cleavage '…wrap?'

Claudia's chin rose. 'No.'

'Don't you think you should?'

Claudia smiled and shook her head. 'You do know I'm not six years old any more, right?'

Luke blinked as she swept past him and headed for the lift, the dress clinging to every microscopic movement of her body. The palm that had held the softness of her breast tingled.

'I'm hardly likely to forget in that outfit,' he called after her.

Luke's breath hitched as Claudia looked over her shoulder at him and gave him a wink.

They ate a sumptuous meal in the aptly named Rumba Room and Claudia was pleased that Avery had thought to book one of the tables that ringed the large dance floor. The entertainment here was always spectacular and being this close they wouldn't miss any of the acts.

The restaurant was crowded and the food was delicious. Avery and Jonah were happy to lead the conversation and Claudia let them go. She spoke where required, as did Luke, but neither of them were very engaged. Claudia was too aware of the strange vibe between her and Luke. He brooded away in her peripheral vision, also responding perfunctorily to verbal cues in between glaring at any man who dared look at her.

It was off-putting to start with but after a couple of glasses of wine Claudia actually started to enjoy it. It was a fairly pointless exercise but knowing that he found her attractive after years of secretly drooling over him was something of a head swell.

And he was looking particularly dashing tonight. He'd teamed a pair of dark trousers with a retro button-up shirt in a paisley print of dark greens, purples and greys. It was open at the neck and the sleeves were rolled up to his elbows and it had been left hanging out.

It was very funky. *Very London.*

His whiskers had been shaved to within an inch of their lives and while she wished he'd just let them grow, become the shaggy and scruffy stubble of her fantasies, a part of her was just as attracted to the whole *London suit* thing he had going on.

She wanted to reach out and feel for herself that a man's face *could* be that deliciously smooth. Trail her finger along his chin. Push her nose into the underside, where neck met jaw, and rub her lips against all the satiny smoothness she knew she'd find there.

And then maybe she could get a better whiff of his sweet but spicy aroma. She'd been trying to place it all night. Not that she was a connoisseur of men's aftershave but she did appreciate a man who smelled good.

'I thought your ambition was to have your own agency by now, Luke?'

Claudia sensed Luke tensing beside her and tuned back into the conversation. What was Avery saying?

'So it was,' Luke said, his lips tight. 'And if it hadn't been for Philippa screwing me over, I would have.'

It was Claudia's turn to tense at the mention of Luke's ex-wife. She held her breath and waited for him to elaborate, to talk more about what must have been a fairly low point in his life. To tell them something about his ex-wife. The mysterious Philippa.

She'd never once had a conversation with him about the woman who had, according to Gloria, broken her son's heart and almost destroyed his professional reputation. One minute he'd been married at a London register office without bothering to even tell his mother and the next it was all over.

Two years was all it had lasted. He'd been going to bring Philippa out to meet them all but they were always too busy and it had never eventuated. And then it had all fallen spectacularly apart.

'Oh, I'm sorry, Luke,' Avery said as Jonah frowned and almost imperceptibly shook his head at Avery. She reached out to touch his hand. 'That was insensitive of me.'

'It's fine,' Luke dismissed. 'I'll get there again. I plan to be out on my own—*completely on my own this time*—in two years.'

Jonah nodded at his friend. 'Well, you can have my account,' he said. 'I haven't been happy with my advertising mob for a while now.'

Luke chuckled, his taut muscles relaxing. 'Well, I'm flattered but you can't just hand over a huge account like that,' he said. 'What if you don't like what I can do?'

'Can't be worse than I have now. I've been a little distracted lately,' he murmured, trailing his finger up Avery's arm, 'to care. I've really let the ball drop in that department. Besides, you forget, I know what you can do with that awful plastic-cheese crap. If you can sell that you can sell anything.'

The whole table laughed this time and Luke joined in. He'd won a national jingle competition when he'd been eleven years old, not long after his parents had partnered with Claudia's to run the Tropicana. It had been to sell pre-wrapped cheese slices and he'd been hooked on advertising ever since.

Luke shrugged. 'I can have a look if you like.'

Jonah nodded. 'That would be good.'

The long, low sultry note of a saxophone oozed out then, interrupting their conversation, and a murmur ran around the room. Claudia felt her heart flutter a little.

Bring on the dancing.

Spotlights from up above flicked on, one at a time, illuminating circles on the dance floor; other instruments joined the saxophone until a raunchy tune was playing.

'The samba,' Claudia announced to no one in particular.

And then a half-dozen couples twirled onto the floor from the wings. The women were dressed in tight, sequined dresses with huge slits that fitted like a second skin and the men were dressed in skinny trousers that fitted across narrow hips, formed a sash across flat abs and flared slightly at the hem. Their white silky shirts bloused and flapped, a little like pirates', the buttons mostly undone.

They found their positions and, as one, they all commenced dancing.

Really dirty dancing.

Bumping and grinding. Big male hands all over petite, scantily clad, female bodies. Spanning waists, gliding down legs, skimming breasts.

They twirled and turned and practically floated across the dance floor, light as feathers. When the music ended, the male dancers dipped their partners with dramatic flair, the spotlights cutting out, and the room burst into applause.

'There's Raoul,' Avery called across the table, raising her voice to be heard over the clapping.

Claudia nodded. She'd noticed. And he'd noticed her too, giving her a quick wink as he'd sambaed past earlier. He'd be over when he finished his set.

Luke frowned. *Raoul.* His eyes searched the dance floor for the man that Avery and Claudia were talking about as the lights came back on again and the dancers started up a tango. He spent the next fifteen minutes checking out each of the incredibly talented dancers wondering who the mysterious Raoul was. And what his relationship to Claudia might be.

He didn't have long to wait.

As the performers finished their last dance they all split up and headed for the tables, cajoling people to dance with them. A tall, dark-haired man with very white teeth, a perfect tan and designer three-day growth made a direct bee-line for Claudia.

Raoul, he presumed.

CHAPTER TWELVE

CLAUDIA STOOD AS Raoul approached. It had been such a long time and she'd missed watching him dance. He had the swagger that all good-looking men possessed and combined it with that loose-hipped sway of a dancer. And it would have been quite something had Claudia not known that Raoul was aware of every single pair of female eyes following him across the floor.

He was beautiful and he knew it.

Sure, Raoul was great to dance with and a fun occasional lover but Claudia had never entertained anything serious with him. When—if—the big L happened *she* wanted to be the centre of that man's world. She needed a man who loved her more than he loved himself.

She *deserved* that, damn it.

Claudia was hyperaware of Luke's gaze on her as Raoul closed the distance between them and swept her into his arms.

'Raoul,' Claudia exclaimed. 'It's so good to see you again.'

Raoul slid a hand onto her waist as he kissed both of her cheeks. '*Mi querida*. You look *magnifica*,' he said, then stood back slightly to admire her dress.

Claudia knew that Raoul's Spanish accent could be used like a lethal weapon on unsuspecting women but she also knew it came and went with remarkable ease. But she didn't care—not tonight.

Luke clearly did though. She could feel the disapproval radiating off him in waves and she felt just a little triumphant.

'You like?' she asked, performing a sexy pivot from side to side for full effect, flirting just a touch.

'You make all the men go a little crazy here tonight, I think.' He grinned. 'What you say, Miss Avery?' he asked.

'Definitely.' Avery smiled as she greeted Raoul. He held out his hand and she placed hers inside, grinning when he kissed it.

'Raoul,' Jonah said, half standing as Raoul's attention shifted and the two men shook hands.

'And who do we have here?' Raoul asked as his gaze came to rest on Luke.

'This is Luke,' Claudia said, jumping in before Luke, who didn't look inclined to chit-chat, could say anything abrupt. 'Raoul's company runs our Latin dance classes and Latin nights at the Tropicana,' she said.

She thought it was best not to introduce Raoul as her lover, no matter how much she wanted to make Luke squirm. Truth was it had been too long to claim him as that any more.

'Ah,' Raoul said. 'This is the famous Luke.' He held out his hand. 'Nice to finally meet you. I have heard much about you.'

Luke vaguely remembered now seeing Raoul at a function when he'd come back last year to work out what they were going to do about being handed the management of the resort. He shook the other man's hand when what he really wanted to do was to demand that *Raoul* remove his other hand from Claudia's waist.

There was no way that hand said anything other than *mine*.

'Darling,' Raoul said as he dropped Luke's hand and returned his attention to Claudia. 'They're playing a cha-cha. Your favourite.'

Claudia didn't need to be asked twice. Luke might disapprove but she'd been dying to dance the second she'd slipped the gorgeous red dress over her head. And she was going out there to shake her booty with the best dancer in the room.

'Lead the way,' she said, ignoring Luke's glowering, and allowed herself to be swept onto the dance floor.

Luke stood there stewing, watching as the other man walked off with Claudia.

His Claudia.

And he did not like what he saw as the dancing began. The dance floor had cleared a little around Claudia and Raoul as people stopped dancing to watch—consequently he could see every move they made. Thankfully the cha-cha didn't appear to be a dance where the couples got too close and Mr Glitterpants seemed to be all about the rules of posture and body space and maintained his ruthlessly— Luke had seen enough clips from *Strictly Come Dancing* to know that.

But hell, if he had Claudia that close in that dress, the rules be damned.

He shook his head of the useless thought.

'She's good, isn't she?' Avery enthused from across the table.

Luke, who was about ready to gouge his own eyes out, was grateful for the interruption. He turned back around to face Avery. 'Yes, she is. Where'd she learn to dance like that?'

'Raoul taught her.' Avery gave him a wink. 'Private lessons, I think.'

Luke bet he had. His lips tightened. He did not want to think about Raoul and Claudia having private lessons.

'We're going to dance,' Avery said, standing up, Jonah taking her hand and following suit. 'You should ask Claudia to dance.'

Luke shook his head. 'I don't dance.' Not like that anyway.

'Sure you do,' Avery teased. 'All you have to do is hang on tight and shuffle your feet. That's what Jonah'll be doing.'

'You got that right.' Jonah grinned.

The cha-cha music came to an end and another tune

started up. 'Oh, I love this one!' Avery exclaimed and dragged Jonah onto the dance floor leaving Luke to his indecision.

Luke wasn't entirely sure what *this one* was but as Raoul's swivel hips got a bit too near Claudia's it was evidently going to be a lot more up close and personal than the cha-cha.

A little *too* up close and personal for his liking.

Before he knew it he was on his feet and storming onto the dance floor.

Claudia shut her eyes, pleased to be losing herself in the music and the syncopation of the dance. Raoul had taught her all she knew and was an excellent dance partner. Luckily on the dance floor he let all his ego and pretentions drop and just became one with the rhythm. Dancing with him was like dancing with the notes as they floated in the air.

And then Luke came along and ruined it. She heard a firm, 'May I cut in,' and opened her eyes to find Luke tapping Raoul *very* firmly on the shoulder while staring at her.

Raoul, who'd also been lost in the dance, looked momentarily puzzled, but he was much too indoctrinated with the code of the dance floor to deny Luke his request. There was an insane moment when she wanted to cling to Raoul's shoulders and beg him not to leave her.

Luke didn't really want to dance. He just didn't want her to dance with Raoul. In her dress. *With no wrap.*

And there was also something slightly wild about Luke tonight. He didn't look in the mood for anything lighthearted.

But then Raoul was bowing slightly and saying, 'Of course,' and moving away and Claudia was left facing Luke on a crowded dance floor. One hand had slid onto her hip and she couldn't decide if the skin beneath burned or tingled.

'I didn't think you could dance,' she said waspishly.

Luke nodded. 'I can't dance like that,' he said. Raoul was

all about keeping the frame and executing the moves perfectly. He was a dancer.

Luke wasn't.

'But I can dance like this,' he said and yanked her body hard against him.

Claudia gasped at the sudden intimate contact. It was completely out of left-field and she hadn't had time to prepare for the impact. And then he started to move and things rubbed and there was friction and it felt so good—better than any expert dance move Raoul could pull—and she knew he felt it too as his hand tightened on her hip.

She wasn't sure she could do this with Luke. This was twenty years of friendship on the line.

'This isn't dancing,' she murmured, the husky note in her voice cutting straight through the music.

'No. But it's real. It's not some fake display for Raoul to advertise his business.'

Claudia looked up into his face. Way up. She'd forgotten how tall he was. Or at least how much taller he was compared to her. Raoul, for all his Spanish good looks, didn't quite make six foot and she had to readjust her centre.

His smooth jaw was just there and she could smell his spicy-sweet aftershave and if they'd been lovers, God help her, she would have stood on tiptoe and licked from the hollow of his throat all the way to his chin.

But they weren't.

'Why does me dancing with Raoul bother you so much?'

Luke, who had been trying desperately to look anywhere else but Claudia, found himself looking down at her.

A mistake.

Two ripe swells of cleavage greeted him, pushed up and out of the V of her halter dress from the way he was holding her all smooshed up against him.

He wished he knew the answer to her question but all he had were bone-headed Neanderthal reactions. Gut reactions.

Because I can't stand the thought of him looking at your

breasts. Any man here looking at them. I can't stand knowing that he's touched them.

Not when I haven't. Not thoroughly anyway.

Yup. So not going to say that.

He dragged his gaze up to her face, her blue eyes glittering like polished turquoise in the spotlights. 'I don't know why it bothers me,' he said. 'It just does.'

Claudia would have been knocked on her butt had she been sitting near a chair. She hadn't expected such raw honesty from him and she didn't know how she felt. Part of her wanted to run and hide. The other part *really* wanted to lick his neck.

So she did the mature thing: she unlocked her gaze from his, dropping it to the patch of shirt that was right in front of her, and decided to change the subject. She cast around for something that would completely lampoon the warm buzz she could feel gathering down low as the delicious friction between them ramped up.

'Why don't you ever talk about Philippa?'

Luke stumbled slightly at the unexpected question. Bloody hell. She sure knew how to kill the buzz. 'There's nothing to say,' he said tersely, keeping his gaze trained on a spot over her shoulder.

Claudia refrained from rolling her eyes. That statement in itself was a big blaring warning signal to his mental health. 'What happened with you two?'

Luke's jaw. 'I don't really think it's any of your business,' he said.

Thinking about Philippa's betrayal, her infidelity, always left Luke feeling a little emasculated and he didn't need that while dancing with a beautiful woman.

Even if it was Claudia. Who he shouldn't be thinking about in relation to his masculinity.

Claudia fell silent for a few moments and just swayed to the music, but that was worse. Because that left her thinking and her thoughts were far from pure.

Far from sensible.

All she could think about was how her breasts rubbed against his chest, how hard and meaty his shoulder felt in her palm and the crazy thump in her groin as their bottom halves rubbed together and things got a little heated down there.

'You broke your mother's heart, you know?' she said.

Again, another comment out of the blue but it was something she'd always wanted to say to him. Marrying Philippa and not inviting his parents had really hurt Gloria. She'd made a big deal out of being understanding but Claudia had been just outside the door when Gloria had broken down on her mother's shoulder and it had been heart-wrenching to hear.

Maybe it wasn't a fair thing to say but Luke had lived a fairly selfish life for a decade, far away from how many of his decisions had affected them all. Moving to the UK the first chance he got, getting married, not wanting anything to do with the resort.

It was his life and these were his decisions to make but they still had an emotional ripple effect.

Luke kept his eyes firmly fixed over her shoulder. 'When I moved to London? I know.'

Claudia shook her head. 'No. When you married Philippa and didn't invite her to the wedding.'

'What?' Luke forgot about not looking at her as he searched Claudia's face, forgot about dancing. 'We didn't invite *anyone* to the wedding. It wasn't a...*wedding...*' he spluttered, 'with the dress and the cake and the...other stuff. It was a quick trip to the register office in our lunch break then back to work. We didn't even go on a honeymoon for three months.'

Claudia blinked at him and barely managed to suppress a shudder. It sounded horrible. No wonder Philippa had left him. She'd known exactly the kind of wedding she wanted from the age of six. A full-on romantic affair on the beach just outside their doorstep and a huge reception at the Tropicana.

'You know your parents would have travelled halfway round the world to be there with you when you got married regardless of how you chose to go about it.'

A spike of guilt lanced Luke as the truth in Claudia's words found their mark and slashed hard. 'We didn't invite anyone,' he reiterated. 'Not even Philippa's parents.'

Claudia shrugged. 'Okay.'

'Mum seemed okay with it when I spoke to her.'

It had never been his intention to hurt his mother and if he'd had any inkling that would be the outcome he would have paid for them both to fly over.

Claudia rolled her eyes. 'Of course she did, you idiot. You were blissfully happy and she didn't want to burst your bubble or burden you with her disappointment. She's your mother—she was never going to put a guilt trip on you.'

'But I suppose you have no compunction?'

'Strangely enough, tonight I don't, no.'

Luke glared down at her. He knew exactly how she felt. 'It's a strange old night,' he said.

A trill undulated in her belly at the intensity in his gaze. 'Amen,' she muttered.

Their eyes locked momentarily before they glanced away from each other. Luke resumed dancing and Claudia followed suit. He *had* been happy, he remembered. *Blissfully happy.* It seemed like a long time ago now and time had mired it in such bitter memories, but he'd really thought Philippa was the one.

'Maybe that's why it failed…your marriage.'

Luke faltered again slightly but kept going. Dancing with Claudia like this was the sweetest torture. All soft and warm against him despite her sharp tongue and prickles.

'Oh, this ought to be good,' he said derisively. 'Please *do* share why you think my marriage failed.'

Claudia shrugged. 'All women want the fairy tale, Luke.

The dress, the cake, the bridesmaids. Where's the romance in a register office?'

Luke snorted. Not Philippa. Her lack of interest in a big event had puzzled him at the time—most women he knew wanted the fancy party, the whole shebang. But not Philippa. Of course, it had become evident only two years later why she hadn't been bothered.

The bitter memories rose to the surface again and twisted a knife in his gut. 'Dear little Claude,' he said, 'still on board the *Love Boat,* I see.'

Claudia froze as his patronising words slid down her back like cold slime. She'd thought he'd finally seen her as a woman tonight—not some adoring little lapdog that followed him around and hero-worshipped him. Not some silly romantic girl with her head in the clouds.

She stepped out of his arms and glared at him. 'I think I'm done with dancing.'

Luke glared back. 'Me too.'

CHAPTER THIRTEEN

AN HOUR LATER Claudia was still royally pissed off.

Lying on her bed in the dark, her red velvet dress twisted around her, she stewed away like some sappy freaking Cinderella who hadn't got the prince after the clock had struck twelve.

Occasional flashes of lightning from the storm brewing outside slanted into the room in strobe-like bursts, illuminating her misery.

God, maybe she was as pathetic as Luke's words had suggested.

Why weren't life *and love* as simple as *The Love Boat*?

Why, more importantly, hadn't she just kept her big mouth shut? Yes, she'd spoken some home truths, things he'd needed to hear, but who'd died and left her in charge of things Luke should know?

And what on earth had possessed her to spout on about where his marriage had gone wrong when she knew hardly anything about it? In fact, until tonight, all she'd known was the name of his ex and that they'd worked together at the same firm.

She'd seen a photo, of course—a tall, gorgeous, curvy brunette. Worldly and sophisticated. The *exact* opposite of her.

But that was it.

And she'd told Luke it was because their wedding hadn't been romantic enough. She, who had been married exactly zero times, was dishing out marital advice!

Argh!

But, man, he'd been especially…infuriating/sexy/irritating tonight. Coming over all *do you think you should be wearing that?* and treating her as if she were some recalcitrant teenager who needed her virtue protected.

She laughed suddenly at the absurdity of it. Her virtue had been lost some time ago. Ironically on a cruise she and Avery had taken together when they'd been nineteen.

She knew he liked her in the dress. His eyes had practically bugged out of his head, for crying out loud. She knew he'd been aware of the delicious friction between them as they'd danced. So why didn't the jackass just accept it for what it was and let it go?

Smile, dance, flirt a little.

Just because there was an attraction there didn't mean it had to be acted on. They were both adults, for crying out loud—not some hormone-riddled teenagers. Surely they could merely enjoy the buzz?

The fact they were both aware of it, the fact that it was taboo, ramped up the buzz even further. It felt like some delicious, unspoken secret between them. Made it sexier, somehow. Made her insides quiver and her outsides hyper-aware of the way velvet felt against her skin—soft but abrasive at the same time. How it rubbed at her nipples, tickled her belly, smoothed over her hips.

Things shifted inside her and Claudia squeezed her thighs together to suppress the sudden tingle that had started between her legs. She squirmed against the bed to relieve it.

It didn't help.

If anything it reminded her how damn long it had been since anyone had been between her legs and she wished she were someone who could just go out and find anyone to scratch an itch. If she were, she'd march down to that ballroom right now and drag Raoul back to her room.

And he'd come willingly.

But she couldn't lie down with Raoul while Luke was on

her mind. It wouldn't be right. And probably not very conducive to a satisfying sexual experience.

But, God help her, if she didn't have a satisfying sexual experience soon she was going to have to invest some serious cash in a latex boyfriend—the best one on the market.

The phone rang and she groped for it in the semi-dark, snatching it up, pleased to be relieved from having to think about the depressing state of her sex life.

Her *non-existent* sex life.

'Avery, if this is you I hope Jonah is there to protect you because I swear to God I'm going to throttle you. The red dress? Bad idea.'

'It's not Avery.'

Claudia shut her eyes as the deep tones, made even sexier by the touch of English class, undulated directly into her ear.

Damn.

'The red dress wasn't a bad idea.'

She opened her eyes. 'Luke...don't...'

'You looked hot in the red dress.'

Claudia's belly flopped over inside her. 'Luke.'

There was silence for a few moments. 'I'm sorry I was a giant arse,' he said.

'No,' Claudia sighed. 'I'm sorry. I shouldn't have gone on about stuff that was none of my business.'

More silence until Claudia began to wonder if he hadn't hung up or nodded off.

'There's a *Love Boat* marathon on cable.'

Claudia rolled her eyes. 'You're just screwing with me now, right?'

He chuckled and goose bumps marched down the side of her neck and the length of her arm. 'Hand on heart, pinky swear, I'm not. Turn on your TV.'

Claudia reached for the remote, which sat beside the phone. 'Which channel?' she asked as she pushed the power button.

'Two six three.'

Claudia scrolled through until she found the channel and there, before her eyes, was Julie with her clipboard. The electronic guide told her they were running back-to-back episodes until six in the morning.

'I think I've died and gone to heaven,' she murmured.

Luke laughed. 'Tell you what, I have a bottle of wine. How about I come to yours and we watch it together?'

'You hate *The Love Boat.*'

'Consider it my penance.'

'Lying on a pillow-top mattress in a five-star hotel, drinking wine and watching television is penance?'

'I know, right?' he said and Claudia could hear the laughter in his voice. 'I don't know how I'll bear it.'

Lost in the sheer sexiness of his voice all low and smiley in her ear, Claudia didn't say anything for a few moments.

'Oh, come on,' he cajoled. 'For old times' sake?'

Claudia knew that could be dangerous. Wine and nostalgia. *Not a good mix.* But if he was willing to try and put the strange dance-floor incident behind them and get back to where they had been—lifelong friends—then she could at least meet him halfway.

'Okay, a couple of episodes but I'm coming to yours.' At least that way she was in control of the situation. She said how long she stayed and what time she left. And she could leave if things got weird again.

Or if her libido demanded she throw caution to the wind and jump Luke's bones.

'You had to wear the dress?' Luke said as he opened the door to her five minutes later. *Was she trying to kill him?*

'You're still in your clothes,' she pointed out.

'Yes.' But he didn't look like *that* in his clothes. 'I thought you'd be more...casual.'

She shrugged. 'I let out my hair. What did *you* do?'

'I...shaved,' he said.

Claudia snorted. *Of course he had.* God forbid his whiskers should ever poke through his skin. 'Well, it was the dress or my pyjamas.'

Luke stepped aside so she could enter. 'Pyjamas would have been fine,' he said as he watched her velvet-swathed derrière sway enticingly back and forth.

'The dress covers more,' she said.

Luke's eyes stayed glued to her shrink-wrapped butt— technically the dress might have covered more. It did, after all, fall to her ankles, but it left *nothing* to the imagination.

Dear God, in the name of all that is holy, let her be wearing underwear.

'Pull up some mattress,' he said. 'They've just started a new episode. It's one of the Christmas ones. I'll pour you some wine.'

Claudia should have hesitated about lying on his bed, especially with what had happened earlier but, as he said, it was just like old times. Him, her, some ham and pineapple pizza and *The Love Boat.*

'Is there a Hawaiian pizza on the room-service menu?' she asked as she kicked off her shoes and took the unrumpled side of the bed.

Luke laughed. 'Nope. Already looked.'

'It's okay,' she said, her eyes drawn to the flickering television screen, which had been muted. 'I'm too full anyway.'

Luke approached with the glasses of wine. 'Cheers,' he said as he handed one over and they clinked them together.

'Are we supposed to be lip-reading?' Claudia asked as Luke pushed the remote and TV guide aside and got comfortable on his side of the bed.

'I thought we could do that thing you see on comedy shows sometimes, where we make up the dialogue as it goes along.'

'Ha. Funny guy,' she said, reaching for the remote that was stranded in what she supposed was the no-go zone between them and unmuted it.

He chuckled as the volume returned. 'You've seen these episodes enough to know them word for word, surely?'

'Shh,' Claudia said, ignoring his quip. 'I'm trying to listen.'

And after that they didn't really speak much. They passed the odd comment about how dated it seemed and about some of the more lurid seventies and eighties fashion.

Claudia yawned as the credits rolled on the second episode. She'd snuggled down amongst the pillows more and was lying on her side, her head propped on her open palm, her elbow bent. 'I should go,' she murmured.

She was feeling kind of mellow though after two glasses of wine. The lightning had ceded to rain and it beat steadily against the windows lending a cosiness to Luke's easy companionship. It was nice and familiar and Claudia was beginning to think she'd imagined the tension earlier.

This was how she remembered her relationship with Luke—nice and easy. Uncomplicated. Maybe this was all they had? All they were destined to have?

Maybe they were at their best when they were stuck in this *Love Boat* time warp?

'I really should go,' she said again.

But then the opening song finished again and the scene opened with Julie and Gopher chatting. 'Oh, I always wanted them to get together.' She sighed. 'Do you remember?'

'Yeah, I remember,' he said.

'They took their time about it,' she muttered, her gaze firmly fixed on the television.

Luke chuckled and she dragged her eyes off the screen. 'What?' she asked.

'Nothing.'

Claudia shot him a wry smile. 'You hate it, don't you?'

Luke shook his head, his gaze roaming her face. 'I love watching you watch it.'

The comment should have been sweet. Uncomplicated.

But his gaze brushed her mouth and suddenly the nice and easy evaporated.

Maybe this wasn't all they were destined to have...

'Pleased I amuse you,' she said, deciding to just ignore him. She laid her head on the pillow and snuggled in letting *The Love Boat* take her away to a far less complicated world.

Where a woman with a clipboard *could* get her man.

When she woke several hours later the room was darker, quieter. No television to spread a flickering light or fill the room with noise. Only the digital clock numbers cast a pall on the situation.

And the situation was not good. She'd fallen asleep. So had he.

They *really* needed to stop doing this.

She was still on her side but had wriggled right down and her dress had ridden up a little and tangled around her knees. One hand was tucked under her cheek, the other hand was lying palm down on Luke's chest.

He had also shuffled down, lying supine with his head rolled in her direction, both his hands lying loosely beside him. His hair was too short to be rumpled but that wasn't where she was focused. The red glow from the clock drew her attention to his mouth. It illuminated his lips, slack in slumber, and showcased them for what they were—nicely full, perfectly delineated.

Just like the warm muscles she could feel beneath her hand.

Her fingers itched to touch his ruthlessly smooth face. To move along his jaw as if she were reading braille, carefully seeking out any patch that he might have missed with his razor. Even if it was just a single solitary scrape against the pads of her fingers.

His chest rose and fell evenly beneath her palm and she could feel the thud of his heart—sure and regular. The same could not be said for her own. Her pulse tripped madly, knowing this…voyeurism was wrong. Knowing even thinking about touching him was wrong.

Her breath turned ragged at the mere thought of crossing that line. But…

He'd done it to her, hadn't he? Watched her while she'd slept?

Watched. An angel had suddenly appeared on her shoulder. *He didn't touch.*

But you were naked. A devil sat on her other shoulder whispering tempting truths.

And it was true. At least Luke was fully clothed.

That doesn't make it okay, the angel insisted.

Go ahead, it's fine, the devil urged.

Claudia had never been more tempted in her life. It was just a tiny touch to his face, after all. Light as a feather. He was sound asleep. He probably wouldn't even feel it.

And then with no conscious control, her hand was moving anyway. Slowly, tentatively, as if he might wake any second. Her fingers made landfall at hard jaw, the pads practically sliding down the slope of his throat his face was that smooth.

She paused, tensed, waited. Held her breath.

Her heart thundered.

Nothing happened. He didn't move. He didn't shift in his sleep. He didn't wake and demand to know what the hell she was doing.

Claudia eked out a ragged breath that sounded freaking cyclonic in the heavy silence of the room. Then, when she was sure he was staying asleep she trailed her finger from the angle of his jaw to his chin. It was less than a touch, more like a butterfly whisper across his skin, a flutter.

And not a single patch of rough whisker to be found. He was baby smooth, talcum soft. Like his lips. Her gaze zeroed in on the two perfect pillows, illuminated to perfection by the red digital glow.

How many times had she fantasised about kissing that mouth? Too many to count.

And there it was, right in front of her.

Her pulse kicked up another notch as the devil whispered, *Kiss him,* and she contemplated doing just that.

That would *definitely* wake him up.

But what if he rejected her advances? It would be embarrassing and awkward. For a *very* long time. It would probably even kill her. She'd probably die of mortification on the spot.

It would certainly be hard to come back from.

Another sinful whisper. *But what if he doesn't?*

Her finger inched towards his mouth, the very tip lightly touching the bow of his top lip. He shook his head slightly as if a mozzie had buzzed him and Claudia froze. His tongue darted out and swiped along where she had touched. But he settled back to sleep again quickly.

Her heart was beating so loudly now she was surprised it alone hadn't woken him up. Hell, she was surprised it hadn't triggered a tsunami.

The possibilities of what could happen here scared the living daylights out of her—the number of ways he could reject her and crush her spirit made her cringe. But she realised something else as she waited like a scared rabbit in the shadows for her heart rate to settle. In a few short months Luke would be heading back to London, and the thought that she might never get another opportunity to show him how she felt suddenly scared her a hell of a lot more.

Screw it.

And the devil smiled.

CHAPTER FOURTEEN

LUKE DRIFTED UP out of the many layers of sleep to a pair of lips brushing along his. Light and gentle but definitely a mouth. Definitely a kiss. His lips responded on autopilot to the pressure before his brain could compute the facts.

He opened his eyes. Claudia?

'Claude?' he murmured, her lips so close they brushed against each other again.

Claudia pulled back abruptly, clearly startled. 'Oh, God,' she whispered. 'I'm sorry...I just...I...'

Every cell in Luke's body stood to attention. Claudia was kissing him? 'You just decided to...kiss me?' he clarified.

Claudia shuffled away a bit, put some distance between them as she rolled back onto her elbow, propping her head up with her hand. She could feel the heat in her face and was grateful it was too dark to see the resulting pink in her cheeks.

'I'm...I don't know what happened. I was just...no.' She shook her head. 'There are no excuses for it.'

Luke was fully awake now. Claudia had kissed him. A delicious buzz took up residence in his lips as the tension from the dance floor revisited. He rolled up onto his elbow too, facing her, his gaze drifting to her breasts where a decent amount of soft swell made the cleavage interesting.

His breath hitched a little.

His pulse spiked a lot.

'Oh, I don't know,' he said. 'I think I'd like to hear them.'

Claudia swallowed as her nipples hardened beneath his blatant gaze and part of her just wanted to grab his hand and bring it to one of them, feel him squeeze it again as he did that night all those weeks ago now.

But she was in more than enough trouble.

'You're always so…clean shaven…so smooth…I was trying to find out if you'd missed a patch…or something.'

'So, you were checking my *lips* for stubble as well? With…your mouth?'

Claudia cringed at how bad it sounded. She'd known this was going to be humiliating but had that stopped her? No.

Stupid devil.

Stupid. Stupid. Stupid.

'No.' She shook her head. 'Your mouth…God…your mouth…' Claudia shut her eyes. How could she explain this?

Tell him you lost your mind temporarily and apologise, the angel demanded.

Screw that, the devil butted in. *Tell him it looked so goddamn pretty and kissable in the glowing red light.*

Claudia groaned, wishing they'd both shut the hell up.

Luke felt a leap in his belly as the tortured little moan escaped her mouth. Every one of her words had gone straight to his groin and stroked. He wanted to kiss her very badly, to put her out of her misery, but the moment was too drenched in seething sexuality to let her off that easily.

He wanted to hear what she had to say about his mouth. And then he was going to put it on her cleavage and suck her nipples deep inside it.

'My mouth?'

Claudia's eyes snapped open at the prompt that sounded more growl than request. He was really going to make her say it.

'I was…curious, all right? I've thought about it…about kissing it…for ages. And suddenly…there's this devil on my shoulder and it was saying how pretty your mouth looked in the light from the clock and it did…it really did. And then I was…'

Luke chuckled. He was sure she wasn't the first person

to use the-devil-made-me-do-it defence but she sounded so damned confounded by it, he couldn't help but be amused.

And flattered. He was flattered all the way to hell and back.

Yeah…he knew a little about that devil.

Luke reached out, bridging the short distance between them, sliding his hand onto her nape, drifting his thumb up and down. It came into contact with the knot at her neck where the halter straps of her dress tied and it took all his willpower not to undo it.

'How long?' he asked, his gaze dropping briefly to her mouth. 'How long have you wanted to kiss me?'

Claudia knew this was the perfect opportunity to lie. He couldn't see inside her head. He didn't know the truth. She could just say ever since that day you groped me. Or since last week. Or something flip. But his gaze was heavy and it seemed to bore straight to the root of her honesty.

And besides, this seemed a moment for honesty. No matter how much it might come back to bite her in the butt.

She swallowed, her throat suddenly tinder dry. His thumb at her nape was seductive and she fought against the downward flutter of her eyelids.

'Most of my life,' she admitted. It sounded so…desperate said out loud and Claudia wished she could snatch the words straight back. 'Kinda pathetic, huh?'

'No,' Luke whispered. 'Sweet.'

Claudia gave a half snort, half groan. He couldn't have chosen worse words if he'd tried.

Luke felt the sudden tension in her neck. 'What?' he asked.

Her eyes opened fully. 'I'm so sick of being sweet old Claude.'

Luke nodded slowly. 'Okay. So what *do* you want?'

Claudia glared at him. What the hell did he think she wanted? 'I want you to shut up and kiss me,' she said not quite managing to keep her exasperation to herself. 'What do *you* want?'

Luke shook his head. 'Oh, you don't want to know what I want.'

Claudia bristled further. 'I'm not a kid, Luke,' she said, staring at him with as much pissed off in her eyes as she could muster. 'I can handle *whatever* it is you want.'

Luke had had a semi hard-on since waking to Claudia's kiss but now it flowered to its maximum potential at her definitive assertion. He held her blazing gaze for a moment before dropping his to her mouth, her breasts, her belly.

'I want to rip this damn dress off you and feast on your breasts while I bury myself inside you. I want to make you come loud enough for Jonah and Avery to hear four floors away. And when I've done that I want to do it all again. I want to do it with you. All. Night. Long.'

Claudia wouldn't have thought it possible for her throat to get any drier—she was wrong. Every cell in her body practically went into a dehydrated torpor at his frank gaze and his even more frank admission.

'Well,' she said, licking her lips as she finally found her voice. 'How about we start with mine and graduate to yours?'

Luke smiled at her then and she smiled back. 'Good answer,' he muttered before closing the distance between them and claiming her mouth.

And claim it he did. Deep and hard, no finesse, no gentle initiation, it was full-on from the second their lips touched. Masterful and demanding, explosive and searing, sucking away her breath and her very ability to reason. It spoke of lust and longing and desires too long denied. It commanded capitulation and she submitted eagerly.

'God,' he groaned against her mouth. 'I want you.'

And before she even had a chance to answer he rolled her onto her back and then he was over her and then on her and he was kissing her again. Deep, wet, open-mouthed kissing, pushing her into the mattress with every thrust of his tongue, kissing her into the bed.

Kissing her into oblivion.

Claudia was finally able to grab a breath when he freed her mouth from his onslaught, but it was only brief before he sucked it away again as he set about kissing a wet trail down her throat and into her cleavage. He swiped his hot tongue along the exposed swells of her breasts and Claudia moaned.

'Undo your top,' he said, his breath ragged. 'I need to look at you.'

Claudia's fingers shook from desire as she lifted her arms to do his bidding. She didn't think to protest his command—because it *had* been a command—she just did it. She wanted him to look too. Hell, she wanted him to do a lot more than that.

She needed him to.

Finally her fingers managed the task and she was pulling her top down, exposing herself to his gaze. His satisfied hiss went straight to her nipples, hardening them before his eyes, and then he was feasting on them, exactly as he'd told her he wanted to, and Claudia was reduced to a mass of cries and moans and pleas not to stop as he lashed the sensitive tips with his tongue and sucked them both in turn deep into his mouth, going from one to the other until she'd lost all powers of higher thinking and just lay there in a sexual bubble where the only thing that existed was his mouth on her breasts.

Not even his hand sliding down her body and back up under her dress registered above the sensations he was creating with his tongue. And then he slipped a hand inside her pants, slid his fingers right into all the slickness and went straight for her clitoris.

The bubble burst.

'Luke,' she cried out, grabbing his shoulders as her body bucked and she felt as if she were falling. Her eyes flashed open.

'Shh, shh,' he murmured against her mouth, kissing her

long and deep and wet again as his fingers stroked her. 'You taste so good,' he whispered before returning to her breasts to feast again.

Claudia's eyes practically rolled back in her head as his fingers circled and rubbed and his tongue swiped and flicked, both of them setting a rhythm that complemented the other, both of them rocking her, pushing her, dragging her, driving her closer and closer and closer to nirvana.

And she was powerless to resist. She wasn't even in her own body any more; she was floating above it somewhere watching herself as all the pieces of her started to come apart. As sensation swelled in her belly and something tore deep, deep, deep inside her, ripping her open, shredding her apart as it swelled further, growing and growing and growing until it was unbearable, a pleasure so painful her body was begging for it to take her, consume her.

And then it did.

'Luke!' she cried out as it claimed her, breaking over her in an almighty shock wave that arched her back, squeezed her buttocks and stiffened her limbs.

'It's too much,' she gasped as it bucked and writhed through her like some kind of possession, like the serpent itself. 'I can't,' she said, fearing she would die as it broke over her again and again, dragging her breath from her lungs, pounding her heart in her chest. But it went on and on shifting and changing, stroking her body with a thousand carnal caresses.

And it *wasn't* too much and she *could.*

And as it started to ebb she reached for it again, crying out for more. She didn't want it to stop. She *never* wanted it to stop. She wanted Luke, his mouth at her breasts, his fingers *exactly where they were*, like this *for ever.*

And he didn't falter, he didn't lift his head or shift his hand, chasing the tail of the orgasm as she moaned and whimpered, quivering through the dying vestiges, wringing out every drop of pleasure.

They were both breathing hard when Claudia finally stilled, Luke collapsing against her, his forehead on her chest, his lips grazing the skin that lay over her heart.

'Are you okay?' he asked, his voice drunk on a sexual high.

Claudia shook her head. No. She was never going to be okay ever again. She felt as if she'd been picked up and shaken and all the cells in her body had fallen out and been put back together in a completely new way. Her heart beat like a drum and her blood surged through her head in painful intensity.

'Oh, my God,' she said, 'I think I just blew a blood vessel in my brain.'

Luke chuckled. His head pounded pretty hard too. He kissed her chest, then all the way up her throat to her mouth where he kissed her gently, reverently, and she sighed against his mouth and he kissed her more just to hear it again.

'I hope you can replicate that,' she said when he finally pulled away.

Luke chuckled. 'Repeat performances are my speciality.'

Claudia's fingers caressed his nape, brushing against his collar. 'God, I'm sorry, you're still fully clothed.' She cringed thinking about how she'd just lain there and let him *do* stuff to her. 'I'm not usually a starfish, I promise. I just...I think you put me into some kind of...stupor.'

'Good.' Luke kissed her brief and hard. 'That was the objective. Besides, you're not exactly naked either.'

Claudia looked down at herself. Her top hiked down, her skirt hitched up. 'I think we should do something about that, don't you?'

Luke grinned. 'Absolutely,' he said as he kissed her nose then eased off her, swinging his legs over the side of the bed and pushing to his feet. 'Take that dress off,' he said as his fingers made short work of his buttons.

Claudia didn't have to be told twice. It wasn't exactly an easy task lying on the bed trying to wriggle out of a dress that was already a twisted, hot mess, especially when she couldn't drag her eyes off Luke's mad scramble to lose his clothes. In fact she stopped altogether when he got down to his undies that were stretched to their limit by a very impressive erection.

Captain Sexypants indeed.

Luke glanced at Claudia as he hooked his thumbs into the waistband of his underwear. The dress still covered her legs.

'I swear if you don't take that thing off soon I'm going to rip it off.'

Claudia shivered at the silky undercurrent in his voice. Her gaze dropped to the hard ridge of his erection. 'I'm sorry,' she said, her belly twisting as she eyed if off, already knowing it was going to hurt *so damn good.* 'I got distracted.'

Luke grinned as he pulled the waistband out slightly and looked down at what was causing Claudia's distraction. He let it snap back into place. 'None of this until I see more of that.'

He nodded his head in the direction of her semi-nudity. Her dress was skew-whiff, her hair was a blonde mess and there were faint red marks on her breasts where he had sucked with a little too much enthusiasm, but she'd never looked more beautiful.

Claudia kicked free of the dress and reclined against the mattress, her arms above her head, arching her back slightly—he wasn't the only one who could tease. She smiled when he growled at her and said, 'Those too,' pointing to the scrap of red lace, the only thing between her and complete nudity.

A strange moment of modesty besieged her and she hesitated. This was the final frontier.

Oh, for goodness' sake, the Devil hissed, *he had his hands all up inside them less than two minutes ago.*

Claudia had to admit, the devil made a good point.

She held his gaze as she lifted her hips and stripped them

down off her legs. When she was completely bared to his view he dropped his gaze and looked his fill. A flush of heat swamped Claudia's body, head to toe, and took up residence between her legs in the exact spot he had found with his fingers to devastating effect.

'Your turn now,' Claudia said, her voice husky, loaded with anticipation.

Luke was out of his underwear in two seconds flat and it was Claudia's turn to look her fill. And she did. Oh, how she did. He jutted out so thick and proud, she understood why women in times gone by would swoon at the sight of a naked man.

If she weren't a strong modern woman she'd just about swoon right off the bed.

Instead her pulse fluttered, her mouth watered, her belly lurched.

Captain Sexy-no-pants!

Luke watched as Claudia licked her lips and his erection grew harder, tighter and he thanked the hotel gods for mini-bar condoms. He snagged the three-pack off the nearby bench and strode the two paces to the bed. Claudia opened her arms and her legs and he went to her, settling between them, his hardness nudging all her slick heat.

He looked at her for long moments, his hands either side of her face, wanting to tuck this memory away for ever. His eyes roved over her features, mapping every one. Blue eyes, cute snub nose, pointy little chin.

'Hi,' he said after a while.

'Hey.'

And then he kissed her and it was deep and slow and sweet, not urgent and hurried like last time. The kind of kiss that melted from the inside, delivering a long, slow burn. Lethal and sexy all at once. And when she moaned against his mouth and twined her arms around his neck to drag him closer the flame burned brighter.

Luke pulled away slightly, moved his mouth to her cheek,

her neck, kissing his way down, aiming to go much further south than he had last time with his mouth.

But then Claudia was pulling on his shoulders and when he looked up at her she said, 'No. I need you in me. Now.'

Luke grinned. He liked her impatience. 'Soon,' he said, returning to his ministrations.

'No,' Claudia said and Luke glanced up again. *'Now.'*

He smiled as he dropped a kiss to her sternum. 'Claude... I don't think I'm going to last too long.'

That was the whole point of dragging out her pleasure, making it good, making it memorable because he doubted his performance was going to be robust after several years of abstinence and sperm tubules that were about to rupture under the pressure.

Claudia cocked an eyebrow at him. 'And you think I'm going to?'

He grinned at her as he reached for the condoms. 'Hurry,' she whispered and he did, quickly donning one over his still-rampant erection.

And then he was back between her thighs, their hips aligned, and she was wrapping her legs around his waist and saying, 'Now, now,' and it was so easy to slide into all her heat, so easy and good and right, easy to pull out and go in again, easy to make her gasp and moan and beg him to not stop, *never stop*, easy to drive them towards the pleasure just a handful of strokes away.

Then they were coming together, gasping and calling out each other's names, rising and rising, holding on tight then letting go and falling, falling, falling.

CHAPTER FIFTEEN

THEY LAY IN silence long after they'd both bumped back to earth. Luke had bundled her close, Claudia's head on his shoulder, her breasts squashed against his ribs, her leg draped across his thighs. And for the longest time they didn't say anything, just drifted along in a delicious post-coital haze.

Claudia supposed she should be feeling some kind of guilt or remorse or mortification but she didn't—not tonight anyway. There would be time enough for recriminations in the days and weeks ahead but for now she was just too damned chilled out. Instead she absently circled a finger around his nearest nipple, enjoying the tickle of the hair.

'You should stop shaving,' she said.

Luke's eyes drifted open. 'No.'

Claudia smiled. 'I like stubble.'

'Then you grow some,' he murmured.

Claudia turned to face him, propping her chin on his chest. 'I remember when you used to look very unshaven and shaggy.'

She lifted her hand and stroked his smooth jawline. God, as a teenager she'd drooled watching him come home from uni all shaggy-haired and scruffy as he headed straight for the beach.

Luke let his eyes drift shut again, enjoying her light caress. 'I lived at the beach, I had to look the part. But I'm a professional working man now and I need to look that part. Shaving *is* London. Stubble is Crescent Cove.'

Claudia sighed, not too far gone to get the message. But

mellow enough to accept it. Accept that, for him, the length of his whiskers defined the type of man he was. 'Whatever,' she murmured. 'You'd still look sexy with stubble.'

Luke smiled. 'I'm sexy enough.'

Claudia smiled too. Arrogant but true. Not that she was going to let him get away with such a cocky statement. 'There's always room for improvement,' she murmured.

Luke opened his eyes and looked directly into hers. 'I know it's trendy these days to look a little ungroomed but a lot of my clients are old school. They respect men who take the time to present well.'

Claudia screwed up her nose. 'Sound like a bunch of old fuddy-duddies to me,' she said, snuggling her head back into his shoulder again.

Luke chuckled at her disdain. Yeah, some of them were but they were also wealthy fuddy-duddies who could afford multimillion-dollar ad campaigns.

They were his fuddy-duddies.

He stroked her hair as his eyelids grew heavy again, enjoying the low-level buzz still undulating through his pleasure receptors and vibrating against his skin.

He was almost asleep when Claudia's quiet, 'So, what did happen between you and Philippa?' drifted his eyelids open. Maybe it was a measure of how relaxed, how ironed out he was that the question didn't particularly alarm him. Earlier he'd told her it wasn't any of her business but now, he wanted her to know.

Maybe it would help her to understand him a little better. Why he was so driven to succeed. Why he'd not had time for the Tropicana. Why he had to go back.

But where to begin?

Claudia waited. He didn't tense as she'd expected him to but it was a long time before he answered and she wondered if he'd gone to sleep.

'She'd gone to Paris for a work conference,' Luke said into the stillness of the night. The pale red light from the clock glowed in Claudia's hair, highlighting the blonde strands, and he played with them absently, sifting through them as he sifted through the memories. 'I was joining her for the weekend. But an opportunity came up and I was able to join her a day early. I thought I'd surprise her. She'd left my key at the desk so I grabbed it and let myself into the room. She was in bed with another man.'

Claudia, who had been distracted by the low sexy rumble of his voice as it vibrated through his ribcage, took a few seconds to process what he'd said. She turned quickly when the implications filtered in, flipping onto her stomach and using her elbow to drag herself closer to him, raising her head and chest above him, looking down into hooded eyes.

'Oh, Luke,' she whispered, stroking her free hand down the side of his impossibly smooth face. 'That's awful...I'm so, so sorry.' She kissed him then, a light press to his lips, to his cheek, to each eyelid in turn. 'I can't even begin to imagine how awful that must have been.'

Luke grimaced as he short-circuited the ugly scene before it played in slow-mo through his head yet again. 'I was... gutted.'

'You had no idea?'

Luke shook his head. 'He was an old lover of hers. Her first boss in advertising at a *very* prestigious, old-school firm. It had apparently been a long-standing arrangement,' he said and even after three years he could still taste the bitterness in his mouth. 'She said it never occurred to her to give him up.'

Claudia could feel his hurt and betrayal, could tell it was still a gaping wound for him. 'I'm so sorry,' she said again, dropping a kiss on his chest because what else could she say?

The angel nodded sagely and reminded her it *was* none of her business. The devil wanted to demand Philippa's address so they could go and scratch the unfaithful bitch's eyes out.

'Oh, it gets worse,' he said. 'Philippa and I were setting up a business on our own. It was all legally binding and set to go. When I dared to express my outrage at her infidelity, when I deigned to separate from her and back out of the partnership, she stole my biggest client, the *firm's* biggest client, right out from under me. Not only could I not go out on my own but the company lost money and took a blow to its reputation. I've spent the last three years trying to repair the mess.'

Claudia thought back to all the uncharitable thoughts she'd had about Luke the last few years and felt ashamed. No wonder he hadn't had any time for her and the Tropicana. No wonder he was looking to hightail it back to London as soon as possible.

'It wasn't your fault, Luke.'

Luke saw the compassion in her eyes; it glittered in the red light that played in her baby blues. 'Maybe not,' he said. 'But I'll always blame myself to a certain degree.'

Claudia couldn't bear the thought of it. 'Why?' she demanded quietly, cupping both of his cheeks in her hands. 'Because you loved someone and trusted them?'

'Yes,' he said, looking directly into her eyes. 'And I'll never be so foolish again.'

Claudia wanted to weep then. Not only had Philippa destroyed his faith in himself and his reputation at work but she'd also ruined him for love.

Ruined him for her.

She didn't know what to do or say to make it better or convince him that one stupid woman did not represent all women. That people did love and it was true and deep and honest. That it could be abiding and faithful. Because he knew that anyway.

He only had to look at his parents, or hers, to truly know that.

But one look at him now, his brown eyes practically glowing with indignation in the red light, she knew he didn't think it applied to him. That he'd shut himself off from the possibility altogether.

And her heart broke into a thousand pieces. Because *she* wanted to be the one to show him what kind of a woman he needed. Show him what love could be.

Because, God help her, she loved him.

She loved a man who could never love or trust again.

The words trembled on her lips but she lacked the courage to say them. Their relationship had taken a huge U-turn tonight and she didn't know where it was going to go from here—nowhere, she suspected—but it certainly wasn't the time to declare her love.

Especially to a man who had just told her he wasn't going there again.

Maybe it had even been a warning.

So she did the only thing she could think of—she rolled up on top of him, straddled his hips and kissed him. Long and deep and slow. He groaned as she pushed her tongue inside his mouth and she moaned back when he grabbed her naked butt and held her firm against his burgeoning erection.

Her pulse sped up, her breathing roughened.

So did his.

Then she kissed his face and his neck and his chest. She swirled her tongue around his nipples before drifting it down to his abs and then his belly button. His hardness pressed into her breasts and she rubbed them against him as she swirled her tongue lower.

The gasp he gasped when she fitted her mouth around him went straight to the hot tingle between her legs. He was as big and thick in her mouth as he had felt inside her and she took as much of him as she could.

'Claude!' he cried out as he buried his hands in her hair.

She let her tongue move all over him, up and down, round and round, finding his sensitive spots and then torturing them ruthlessly with the kind of tongue lashing he'd given her breasts earlier.

He groaned again, his hands leaving her hair to fist in

the sheets. 'If you keep doing that,' he panted, 'it's going to end real soon.'

Claudia could feel the tension in his thighs, his buttocks, see the whites of his knuckles. A sense of power washed through her as the tingling between her legs intensified to an excruciating level and she knew there was only one way to relieve it.

Her mouth released him and he groaned. Whether it was in protest or relief she wasn't sure. She just knew she had to feel all that wonderful hardness deep inside her, to the hilt, right up where that damn tingle had a stranglehold.

She dragged her way back up his body, grabbing handfuls of his flesh to assist her. When she reached her destination she straddled him again then leaned over, reaching for a condom from the bedside table. He tried to curl up, take a nipple into his mouth but she swatted him back down.

'No,' she said, because she knew how that went and before she knew it she'd be a drooling, boneless starfish all over again when what she needed was to dominate.

Not be passive.

Relieve the unbearable tension and show him with her body, if not with her words, that she was his.

'Keep your hands exactly where they are, mister.'

'Ooh, bossy.' He grinned, planting his hands firmly on her hips.

Claudia didn't bother to answer, she just tore the foil wrapper with her teeth, reached for him and rolled it on as if she'd worked in a condom factory all her life. And then she was positioning herself over him and then, slowly, sinking down.

'Oh, God.' Luke's groan matched her own as his fingers dug into her hips.

Claudia shut her eyes and threw her head back as she seated herself on him, completely impaled, the tingles obliterated. She was right—it *did* hurt so damned good.

When she opened her eyes again he was watching her,

his hands still firmly planted on her hips. 'What now?' he murmured.

'This,' she said, circling her hips, once, twice, three times, panting with the stretch and fullness of it. 'And this,' she said, leaning forward, placing her hands on his shoulders and slowly, very slowly easing herself off him all the way then sinking back down again.

Luke groaned as his groin leapt and his mouth watered. Her breasts were glorious, pert and swaying enticingly before him. 'Again,' he said, their gazes locking.

She did it again. And again. And again. He groaned all three times but his eyes didn't leave her face.

'You know,' she said as she lifted off all the way for the fourth time, 'not all women are like...' she pushed back onto him again, sinking to the hilt again '...her.'

Claudia almost said her name but she didn't want the ugliness of what she'd done to intrude on this moment.

She didn't want Philippa in *their* moment.

Luke nodded. 'I know,' he panted as his body fought to contain the gathering storm seething in his groin.

'Do you?' she whispered as she slid up again, fighting to keep her eyes from rolling back in her head. To keep them open. To keep them on him.

'Yes,' he hissed as he thrust up hard to meet her this time, holding her hips tight. The violent jiggle of her breasts and her gasp, deeply satisfying.

Claudia shut her eyes briefly as the friction turned to something else, something pulsatile. She opened them and looked straight at him as she lifted her hips one more time. 'I would never do that to you.'

Even though they could never be, she needed to know that he knew that.

Luke thrust. 'I know.'

She lifted. 'Do you?'

He thrust. 'Yes.'

Claudia groaned as the tingling returned and the pulses

grew and expanded, spreading from her belly button to her hips, her thighs, her buttocks, and she moved quicker, more urgently, trying to ease the glorious burn, not able to talk any more, only able to move up and down, up and down, up and down.

If she talked she might just say too much in this state of sexual insanity.

Luke sensed her urgency, felt it echo deep inside himself. He met her stroke for stroke, her lovely breasts taunting him with each one, giving her what she didn't even know she wanted, as his own orgasm pulled at his self-control, pulsing up from the root of his erection, fraying the world around him and when he couldn't take it any more he curled up, sliding his hands to the small of her back and sucking a nipple deep into his mouth.

'Luke!' she cried out, spearing her fingers into his hair, adjusting to their new position easily, riding him without missing a beat.

'Yes,' she said, 'yes, yes, yes.'

And then they both shattered together.

CHAPTER SIXTEEN

THE TELEPHONE JANGLED right near her ear the next morning dragging Claudia out of the deepest depth of slumber with all the finesse of a jackhammer. She reached for it automatically.

'Hello?' she mumbled, her heart racing.

'Claude?'

Avery? 'Yes.'

'What are you doing in Luke's room at six in the morning?'

Claudia's heart raced a little more as her surroundings filtered in. Same-looking hotel room as hers but this one had the addition of a large naked man spooned around her, his hand low down on her belly, his mouth pressed to her shoulder blade.

Last night. Luke's apology. A bottle of wine.

The Love Boat.

The love*making.*

Crap.

'Oh…er…we were just…having another…planning meeting…' Claudia winced at the obvious lie.

'You sound like I've just woken you up,' Avery said, her voice laced with scepticism.

'No, just tired,' Claudia assured and faked a yawn. 'Didn't really sleep much last night.'

And that *was* the truth. They'd been awake long enough to use the third condom before falling into an exhausted heap together.

'Well, you're supposed to be down here with us having breakfast, remember? We have to leave at seven-thirty.'

Claudia stifled a groan. She remembered. She'd only agreed to come away if they got back as early as possible on Sunday morning so they could have everything shipshape for the reopening of their doors on Monday.

But that was before her and Luke's wild, three-condom sexual spree. 'Sorry. Give us ten minutes. We'll be straight down.'

Claudia hung up. 'Let me guess,' Luke said in his deep voice, all sexy and rumbly from sleep. 'Avery.'

'Yes.' His hand moved from her belly to her breast, his lips buzzed her neck and Claudia shut her eyes briefly as her body flowered beneath his touch. His thumb grazed a nipple and it felt so damn good.

But they didn't have time for this.

'No, stop,' Claudia said, scrambling out of bed, far away from his magical mouth and his sinful hands. 'We have ten minutes to get down to the dining room,' she said, hunting around for her clothes.

Luke watched the view as she bent over to pluck her discarded clothes off the floor. Predictably, his body stirred.

'Don't just lie there,' she said as she threw her dress over her head, not bothering with her underwear, and his stirrings turned to a full-blown erection at the thought of her being completely commando. 'We have eight minutes to get to the dining room and I need to go and get changed.'

'Can't,' he said. 'Not yet. I have this swelling problem.' He peeled back the sheet to show her.

Claudia swallowed as her gaze zeroed in on him. *Dear God.* He was magnificent. Thick and large. His erection dominated the flatness of his belly with its potency.

Luke hardened further at her frank appreciation. 'Maybe you could help me with it?'

Claudia almost groaned out loud. If only she hadn't been so bloody gung-ho about getting back to Crescent Cove,

Avery wouldn't have rung trying to find her and she could have all that magnificent male hardness inside her right now.

Claudia shut her eyes to block out both the mental and *actual* picture. 'I doubt it's terminal,' she said as she turned her back on him, stuffing her feet into her shoes. 'Seven minutes.' She grabbed her key off the nearby bench. 'See you down there.'

And she didn't look back no matter how tempted she was. And she was very, very tempted.

How she got through the remainder of the day, Claudia didn't know. She felt as if she had a huge, flashing, neon sign above her head saying 'look at me, look at me, I had hot dirty sex last night with someone I shouldn't have'. So she was brighter, chirpier, she worked harder, she walked faster, she knocked herself out playing the best, brightest version of herself she could muster after a night of head-banging sex and only two hours' sleep.

In fact she might have overdone it slightly if people's concerned faces were anything to go by. 'Are you okay?' Avery had finally asked her around mid-afternoon. 'You seem kind of...wired.'

Claudia had nodded vigorously. 'Fine and dandy,' she'd chirped, 'Just excited about tomorrow,' and she had buzzed off to attend to something else.

But by the time night rocked around again and she finally retired to her room about nine o'clock she was utterly exhausted and ready to drop. She collapsed back on her bed and lay there for a few moments like a starfish.

But then that got her thinking about Luke. About lying passively, while he turned her into a drooling mess, bringing her to orgasm with his hand and his mouth. A familiar tingle started up again and she rolled on her side, stuffing a fist between her legs to ease the ache.

Maybe her body knew somehow, could sense that he was just in the next room, or maybe it was the delicious waft of

Luke, of their sex, washing over her. With no time to shower this morning she'd been smelling Luke on her all day—earthy and male and very hard to ignore.

She'd been semi turned on all day.

Of course she could have had a shower when she'd ducked up to her room to change into her uniform when they'd first arrived back but, perversely, she hadn't wanted to wash him away.

She'd wanted to savour it, savour him, for a bit longer.

The way she'd savoured the smiles he gave her whenever she caught him looking at her. Those dirty smiles. The kind of smile that said, I know what you look like naked and screaming my name.

She wanted to savour every moment because if getting the Tropicana opening-ready today while he spent half the day talking into his Bluetooth had taught her anything, it was that she belonged here and his life was on the other side of the world.

Whatever had happened between them she couldn't forget that.

So, she loved him. That was both a revelation and not. She'd always loved him. It was just the first time she'd admitted it to herself. But it didn't change things. She wasn't going to go halfway around the world for a guy who didn't love her back. A workaholic divorcee whose career was his number one priority. A guy who was determined to never be so *foolish* again.

And if he loved her back, if he asked her to go with him…?

Best not to build those kinds of castles in the sky. They hadn't yet talked about what had happened or said anything, for that matter, of a personal nature to each other all day. It would have to come, she knew, but for now she was just going to savour the memory.

The knock on the interconnecting door a minute later surprised the hell out of her and she sprang off the mattress, her heart racing. The last thing she needed was to be horizontal around Luke again.

'Come in,' she called as she stood awkwardly at the foot of the bed, self-consciously checking her hair was still up in its ponytail.

The door opened and she smiled at Luke, who entered very hesitantly. 'Hi,' he said.

'Hey.'

They both smiled as they remembered the last time they'd done this routine—naked and plastered together in a Cairns hotel room. Then, as if they'd both realised it wasn't an appropriate thought to have, their smiles faded simultaneously.

'I thought we should probably talk,' Luke said.

Claudia nodded. 'Yes...I guess.'

'You don't sound too sure.'

She shrugged. 'At the moment denial is looking pretty good.'

Luke chuckled. 'That's an option.'

Claudia laughed too, grateful for the easing of tension. 'You want a beer?' she asked.

'Sure,' Luke said. 'Thanks.'

Claudia was grateful for something to do with her hands other than option A, which was to put them all over him. He was wearing boardies and a T-shirt again and Claudia couldn't help but be aware of what easy access that was. She reached into the mini-bar and pulled out a frosty bottle and handed it to him, then poured herself a glass of wine from the half-empty bottle sitting in the door of the fridge.

One of the advantages to being the boss—free mini-bar.

Normally she'd have clinked her glass to his bottle but keeping a distance between them seemed wise. Taking a sip, she leaned back against the bench, the fridge door cool on her calves.

'So where *do* we go from here?' she asked.

Luke shrugged. 'A part of me wants to suggest that we

accept it happened and move on. Never mention it again. Never…go there again.'

Claudia swallowed as his words cut her to the quick. His eagerness to move on hurt. Despite telling herself not to she *had* been spinning castles in the air. Fantasising about him saying, 'I'm giving up London for you.' But she knew it was the only thing that made sense for two people with very different life goals.

'That's probably the wisest thing,' she said.

Luke nodded. 'Wise, yes.'

But Claudia didn't think his heart sounded in it and a tiny spark of hope flared to life. 'What about the other part of you?' she asked.

Luke took a swig of his beer. She so *did not* want to know about *that* part of him. 'I tend not to listen to that side,' he dismissed.

Which was a lie of course. That was his maverick side, his throw-caution-to-the-wind side. The creative part, the part that made him a gifted advertising executive, that formed new and innovative ideas that clients went nuts over.

He indulged that side all the time. Just *not* this time.

Claudia scrunched her nose. She wasn't a fan of the first option so she was willing to take anything on board. 'I still think it should get a vote.'

'Oh, no.' Luke shook his head. 'It definitely should not get a vote.'

'Oh, really? Why not?'

'Because that part wants to rip that awful uniform off you and spend all night making you come.'

Claudia stilled. How could a statement so blatantly dirty sound so posh? 'Oh.'

Luke took another swig of his beer. 'Yes. Oh.'

Claudia's hand trembled a little as her insides tied themselves into a massive knot. She placed her glass on the bench beside her, not trusting herself to keep hold of it as she slowly lost her grip on the real world.

'I could be…' she cleared her throat '…amenable…to that.'

Luke did not need another invitation. On a muffled expletive he closed the distance between them, sliding his beer onto the bench beside her wine before grabbing her around the waist, yanking her in close to him and slamming his mouth down onto hers.

And it didn't disappoint. 'God,' he groaned as his mouth lifted to kiss her cheek, her eye, her ear. 'I've been fantasising about this all day.'

Claudia went up on her tippy toes, clutching him around the shoulders, hanging on as his lips ravaged her neck, bending her back for better access as he swirled his tongue down into her cleavage. 'Luke,' she gasped as his hand yanked her blouse out of her skirt then glided up underneath, up, up, up to claim a breast, squeezing and kneading, rubbing across the aching tip with devastating effect.

'We could keep doing this,' Claudia said as Luke's mouth trailed a wet trail along a collarbone.

'Right,' Luke panted as his mouth trekked back down her chest. He yanked her bra cup aside and her long low moan was like music to his ears. 'We're mature adults—we can handle a temporary…thing.'

Claudia nodded then gasped as Luke's mouth found her nipple. 'Oh, God.'

'I don't want to stop this,' he murmured in between wet swirls around her nipples. 'Do you want me to?'

Claudia shook her head. 'No,' she said, her denial husky but no less forceful. She really didn't. Even if it was going to leave her crushed into the ground at the end, she'd take whatever he could give her here and now, because if she couldn't have all of him then she'd have this time and tuck it inside her for ever knowing at least she had loved once upon a time.

Luke smiled and swirled his way back up to her neck, her mouth. 'Good.' He grinned, cupping her cheeks, his mouth on hers. 'So good.'

And then he kissed her again, long and slow, savouring every delicious second, revelling in the knowledge that her kisses were going to be part of his life for the foreseeable future. Before coming back to Cairns the thought of giving one woman such power again would have scared the bejesus out of him but Claudia was right—all women weren't the same and she was no Philippa.

He pulled back slightly, breathing hard. 'Why aren't we horizontal?' he murmured.

She grinned. 'I have no idea. We should do something about that.' And she kissed him again, clinging to his neck as he slowly walked them backwards towards the bed.

But they hadn't gone very far when Claudia's room door opened and Gloria and Lena walked in. Claudia and Luke sprang apart as if they'd been hit by a taser. Gloria and Lena's conversation stopped abruptly as they stared open-mouthed at their respective children.

'Oh, Lena,' Gloria gasped, turning to Claudia's mother. 'It's finally happened.'

Lena grabbed Gloria's hand. 'I know,' she said. 'Finally.'

Gloria moved into the room, making a beeline for her son. 'We'd always hoped, didn't we, Lena?' she said. Lena nodded. 'But you went off to London and then you got married and you didn't want to manage the resort with Claude and we thought...well, it looked like it was never going to happen and now...'

Luke watched, horrified, as the two women approached with huge beaming smiles. He glanced at Claudia, who was thankfully covered and looking just as stunned by the events of the last minute. *What a freaking disaster.* Why the hell was her door open? If their mothers had been a minute later God only knew what kind of a state he and Claudia would have been in.

It certainly wouldn't have been vertical.

He cringed thinking about it. It was bad enough standing here at thirty-two, caught with his hands all over Claudia and a raging hard-on in front of his glowing mother; he didn't need to think about how much worse it could have been.

At least kissing was more easily explained. *Hopefully.*

Claudia glanced at Luke as their mothers kept raving about what a wonderful couple they'd always known she and Luke would make. Luke looked as if he was about to throw up.

She knew how he felt.

This was bad. Very bad. Exactly what they'd wanted to avoid—involving two people who wouldn't understand it when Luke left to go back to London.

She had to do something, say something—quick.

'This is not what it seems,' Claudia said.

CHAPTER SEVENTEEN

GLORIA AND LENA stopped talking abruptly and a spike of guilt at bursting their bubble poked Claudia right in the centre of her chest.

'Okay,' her mother said although clearly she didn't believe Claudia. 'What is it, then?'

Good question Luke thought as he glanced down at Claudia. How on earth could either of them explain away what their mothers had seen? *Convincingly.*

'Luke and I were just sharing a good-luck-for-opening-day kiss,' she said.

'That didn't look like a good-luck kiss to me,' Gloria said and winked at Lena.

'It got a little out of hand,' Claudia admitted, 'but we're both exhausted from working so hard and nervous about tomorrow... It was...pure reaction...just one of those strange *isolated* moments that sometimes happen when people work closely together on something and the stakes are high. That's all.'

'That's all?' her mother repeated, clearly unconvinced.

'It happens all the time in advertising, doesn't it, Luke?' she said, nudging Captain *Silent-pants* for help.

Luke nodded. It sounded crazy but maybe they could convince their mothers if they stuck to her ridiculous isolated-reactionary-incident-brought-about-by-exhaustion story. 'That's right.'

'Oh? Kissed a lot of your colleagues, have you?' his mother asked.

Luke cleared his throat. 'Some,' he said lamely. Lying to

his mother was more difficult as a grown man than it had been as a teenager.

'There is absolutely *nothing* between us,' Claudia said. '*Nothing.* Just old friends who let something go too far because we were exhausted and...overwhelmed and it won't happen again, right, Luke?' she asked him.

Luke nodded vigorously. 'It won't.'

Gloria and Lena glanced at each other and grinned a little. 'Okay, sure,' Gloria said. 'That makes sense. A one-off.'

'Won't happen again.' Lena nodded.

Luke narrowed his gaze. 'It won't.'

'Okay, sure,' Gloria said, and Lena nodded her agreement.

Claudia sighed. They both looked suspiciously bright-eyed and Claudia's dismay grew. She and Luke didn't need the pressure of their parental expectations. They both knew nothing short of the royalesque wedding their mothers had *apparently* been planning for the last twenty years would satisfy Gloria and Lena.

Their *thing* was over before it had even begun.

Dead in the water.

'Was there a reason why you barged in without knocking?' she asked her mother.

Lena tutted at her daughter's sass. 'The door was unlocked.'

'I haven't been locking it with the hotel empty.'

'We just wanted to let you both know that if everything goes smoothly the next two days we'll be setting off on Wednesday.'

Luke wanted to say, *And you couldn't use the phone?* but that would be rude and ungrateful and they spent the next few minutes talking over their parents' travel plans as if their mothers hadn't just caught them making out like horny teenagers.

It felt awkward and unnatural and Luke was relieved when Gloria and Lena took their leave. 'Be good,' Lena said as they both walked to the door, springs in their step.

'And if you can't be good, be careful,' Gloria threw over her shoulder as the door slowly closed.

Claudia and Luke stared at the door as it clicked shut on a burst of raucous female laughter and excited chatter they could hear despite the thick wooden barrier. 'Oh, God,' Luke said. 'They're already picking out china patterns, aren't they?'

Claudia nodded miserably. She wondered if her mother or Gloria had any idea that their unintentional interruption had actually had the opposite effect to what they'd clearly been plotting all these years.

'You and I can never just have a...fling, can we?' he murmured.

'No.' Claudia shook her head. 'Not with our parents knowing anyway. If we're in any kind of a relationship, they're going to be sending out invitations and humming the wedding march. But we always knew that...'

'Yes.' Luke rubbed a hand along his neck. *They had.* They'd just let their hormones get in the way.

Stupid!

Look what had happened the last time he'd let them take over—an ex-wife and a torpedoed career. Did he learn nothing?

'We can't do this, can we?'

Claudia looked at him. A quarter of an hour ago she'd been minutes away from having him naked and inside her. Now she knew she'd never know that feeling again and she thanked her lucky stars for last night. To have known Luke in the carnal sense.

'No. We'll break their hearts when you go back to London, back to your other life. I don't want that to be a source of friction between them.'

She waited for him to say he wasn't going to go back. That he'd decided to stay.

Luke shoved his hands on his hips. 'Yes.'

He looked frustrated and weary and Claudia knew exactly how he felt. Their kissing had revved her up and now she was standing here, her engine running, with nowhere to go. 'We'll always have last night.' She shrugged.

Luke gave her a half-smile. 'Yeah,' he murmured, his gaze dropping to her mouth briefly, the muscles in his corded forearms flexing and for a second she thought he was going to leap the distance between them and kiss her anyway.

But he didn't.

Instead he looked away, dropped his hands to his sides and headed for his room. 'See you in the morning,' he said, pulling the door closed after him.

Claudia stared at the door.

Morning.

One long, sleepless night away.

Opening day was a success. Everything went off without a hitch and their guests were all lovely, very aware of the hardship that had recently befallen the Tropicana and extra accommodating with the limited activities available. Mostly they were family groups, grateful for the lower-key atmosphere, happy to hang out at the pool and play on the beach.

On Wednesday their parents left to much fanfare and relief as far as Claudia was concerned. Even just the disappointment she'd glimpsed on her mother's face as she'd realised she and Luke had been serious about their non-relationship had been hard to take.

She couldn't begin to imagine how much worse it would be if they had gone ahead and had a fling, built up their mothers' hopes and dreams only to dash them all when Luke left to go back home again.

Because he *was* going back to London—he'd made that very clear.

Thankfully over the following days and weeks they were much too busy to dwell on it. Between running the hotel and moving things along with the spa complex, not to mention Luke working all hours of the night as well as working with Jonah on a new advertising campaign, they didn't have time to be social.

They didn't have time to be lovers.

Make time, that pesky little devil that seemed to have taken up permanent residence on her shoulder, urged her every night as she lay in bed trying *not* to think about Luke lying in his bed. Right next door. Completely naked.

Sure, she could make the time if she wanted to throw caution to the wind, set up something clandestine with him, but the outcome wouldn't change. He was still leaving and all nights and nights of endless sex and passion would ultimately get her was even more exhausted than she was now.

There was a lot to do and she had to be on her game—not yawning and constantly distracted by whatever acrobatic sex they'd had the night before. Her guests deserved bright, chipper Claudia of old and that was what they were getting. The Tropicana had been dealt a huge blow both physically and financially and turning that around took hard work and focus.

And that was what she chose to concentrate on. Getting the Tropicana back. Salvaging the old reputation at the same time she forged ahead with establishing another—a first-class spa facility with luxury tent accommodation.

Who needed nights and nights of endless sex and passion?

She put Luke and what could have been in a special place to pull out and look at again another day in the future.

Maybe when it had stopped hurting so damn much.

The weeks blended into months and the resort exceeded Claudia's expectations, achieving a seventy per cent occupancy over the winter season. Everyone was busy and it was good to have a cash flow again. They were able to re-establish a lot of activities—lei threading, bush-tucker tours, beachcomber collaging, shell jewellery and ballroom dancing were all added to the programme along with the Saturday night luau. Several regular themed nights—pirate, medieval and mermaids—were held in the dining room with food and entertainment to match, and proved popular with the families.

But the biggest change was the building of the day spa, which they'd decided to call Tropicana Retreat. Thanks to government and tourist-industry pressure on banks, councils and insurance companies, everything had gone through without a hitch and they were able to get the build started within two months.

Claudia had hired a local building company who were surprisingly available given how much of the area needed rebuilding. But so much couldn't be done yet, not until insurance money had come through, so the company had jumped at the chance to create something special at the Tropicana.

Once the work started it took hardly any time to build. It was just a simple rectangular plan with a large open reception area that flowed into a salon area where manicures, pedicures and facials were done. Beyond that were four rooms for massage treatments and another room where a state-of-the-art Vichy shower was installed allowing them to do scrubs and all kinds of body wraps.

The fit-out took longer with Avery and Claudia poring over every single tile, pedicure chair, paint colour and blind-fabric swatch. Claudia was pleased to have Avery and her eye for the exquisite and happy to leave her to it once the big decisions had been made, freeing her up to tackle the hiring of staff.

Luke took on the task of managing the luxury tent accommodation, which, again, wasn't a huge construction job. The wooden platforms were simple and sourcing the right fabric for the tent-like shelter wasn't as difficult as he'd thought. The largest part of the build was the attached luxury bathroom facilities.

Nobody paid a few hundred dollars a night to sleep in a tent to have to go walkabout for a bathroom in the middle of the dark so it was important that they catered for that.

The biggest issue and the one that caused the most debate

was deciding where each of the six tents would ultimately be located on the grounds. They had an enlarged aerial photograph of the grounds as they were now, post cyclone, that Jonah had taken from the chopper, and they used monopoly houses for the tent sites, which they moved around and around trying to choose the best positions.

It was exciting to watch *everything* come together. Claudia felt a renewed sense of pride and vigour in the Tropicana as her dreams slowly became reality.

And if there were times where things were a little tense between her and Luke or she caught him looking at her with such abject hunger she wanted to rip all his clothes off, then knowing they were creating something amazing together, that they were reshaping this wonderful legacy of theirs, helped to temper those times.

They were both doing the right thing with a relationship that was never going to go anywhere so pouring all their sexual energy into the Tropicana made sense.

Indulging would be easy. But the consequences would be hard.

It was better this way.

Two weeks out from the official launch of the Tropicana Retreat, Luke sat at his desk at eleven o'clock at night staring at the email recalling him, in no uncertain terms, to London. The multimillion-dollar account he'd been working on for months was ready to go and the company CEO in question wanted Luke there to do the presentation.

Only Luke.

It was his chance to redeem himself and restore his reputation. And he wanted it.

He *needed* it.

It wasn't as if he were needed here any more with the bulk of the new project complete. Claudia could handle it from now on in. Hell, she'd always been able to handle it.

Damn their interfering parents.

What *he* couldn't handle for too much longer was keeping his hands off her.

Another good reason to get the hell out of Dodge.

She swanned around in that awful uniform that was fast becoming the sexiest piece of polyester in the world, being all chirpy and pleasant and efficient, and all he wanted to do was drag her down behind that reception desk, demand that she open her legs and say, 'Yes sir,' to him, the way she said it to guests.

God, the number of times she'd leaned over that damn map moving a stupid little green plastic house around while giving him a full view of whatever bra she was wearing for the day…

He deserved a medal for not ripping that awful shirt off her and dragging her onto his lap.

At every turn she'd tempted him. Not deliberately, he knew that, but his body just would not listen to reason. He'd taken to running on the beach every morning just to run off his morning erection.

It was that or open the connecting door to their rooms and the consequences be damned.

Even the thought was making him hard, frustration biting deep into his groin. Irritated at himself, at his erection, at the continual sexual fantasies of Claudia, he tapped Qantas into the computer's search engine and looked for a flight leaving asap.

Fifteen minutes later he was booked out at lunchtime tomorrow. And his erection was gone.

Now he just had to break the news to Claudia.

CHAPTER EIGHTEEN

CLAUDIA WAS SITTING cross-legged on her bed cradling a frosty glass of Milo looking at some designs for a new range of Tropicana uniforms that Avery had selected for her to vet. Avery, who had declared the current uniform an unnatural disaster, had been working on Claudia for months now about the need for an update. She'd insisted on a different uniform for the spa—there was no way she was wearing polyester!—and Claudia had agreed.

But changing the Tropicana uniform wasn't such an easy thing for Claudia. She looked down at the shirt she was wearing and at the trousers she'd discarded on the chair by the bed earlier. All she'd ever wanted to do as a girl was wear this uniform and she'd always been proud of it. It was difficult to let go.

But, she had to admit, Avery's choices were quite stunning, remarkably similar in style to the current range of uniform, just some funkier patterns and nicer fabrics.

It was time, she knew, for the Tropicana—and her—to move on.

As she flicked through the catalogue, going from one diligently marked colour-coded tab to the next, she tried not to think about what Luke might be doing next door. She was aware, with the grand opening nearing, that their time was coming to an end.

That there would be nothing to hold him here soon.

The thought was depressing as hell. And what did that say about her? That she'd rather he be here making her miserable every day because she loved him and she couldn't tell him and she couldn't touch him, instead of on the opposite side of the world, which would at least give her aching heart a chance to recover.

Love really was cruel.

She dug a spoon around in the glass, which was more Milo than milk, and stirred it listlessly. Her ultimate comfort drink. Some people chose vodka—she chose a kids' chocolate milk drink. She reached over to the open tin she'd taken from the kitchen earlier and tipped two more spoonfuls into the glass and stirred, watching it as it mixed in, the glass mainly just a thick chocolaty sludge now.

She loaded a spoonful into her mouth and shut her eyes as the sweet crunch appeased her hormones.

She'd been drinking a lot of Milo lately. If she didn't watch it she'd be fat as a house. She looked down at her bare thighs. Was it just her funk or did she have more cellulite lately?

When a knock on the connecting door thundered a moment later she nearly upended the whole glass in her lap from fright. Some of it splashed out and landed on her shirt and flicked onto her neck as the door opened abruptly to reveal a rather brooding-looking Luke.

'I thought we were waiting for *permission* to enter *before* we entered?' Claudia griped as she wiped at the milky chocolate sludge on her neck.

It had been a long time since he'd been in her room and, conscious of her state of undress—and her bare, Milo-cellulitic legs—it was hard not to think about the kiss that had happened last time he'd been here.

The kiss that had almost become so much more.

Luke's breath seized in his chest for a moment. He couldn't believe what she was wearing. Or wasn't wearing, to be more precise. His gaze automatically drifted to her legs, his memory automatically drifting to how good it felt to have them wrapped around his waist.

And not forgetting that sexy awful blue and yellow palm-tree shirt that he'd fantasised about tearing off almost every night for three months.

She had to be wearing that.

'Sorry,' he apologised. 'I didn't think.' And he hadn't. He'd just wanted to come in and tell her he was leaving and get the hell out again.

But here she was. Not dressed to kill, not dressed to seduce, not dressed to attract.

But doing all three anyway.

For God's sake, she had a *milk moustache.* A milk moustache *should not,* in any way, shape or form, be sexy. But, God help him, he wanted to lick it right off her mouth.

'Well? What do you want, Luke?' she asked and he could hear the exasperation and wondered if it was born from the same well of frustration as his was.

He dragged his gaze off her mouth. 'I've booked a flight out lunchtime tomorrow.'

Something resembling a hammer blow hit Claudia fair in the chest at the unexpected news. Her heart beat painfully behind her ribs; a massive lump lodged itself in her throat making it hard to swallow, hard to breathe. She'd known it was happening soon but not this soon.

Not tomorrow.

She gripped the glass and handle of the spoon tight. 'I see.'

'I have to go back for this presentation, for that client I told you about. He only wants me.'

Claudia knew how the mysterious client felt. 'Okay.'

Luke had been prepared for tears and anger but not this quiet, calm acceptance. 'I wouldn't skip out if I didn't have to.' More quiet, more calmness from Claudia. 'It's my career,' he added.

'I said okay.'

The response was snappier and Luke was grateful to see some spark. 'You don't need me here, Claude,' he said gently.

Claudia looked at him, her heart really breaking now. Sure. But what about what she *wanted*?

This was it. He was really going.

'You don't know what I need.'

Luke sighed. She was right—he didn't. And he sure as hell didn't want to go there. It was dangerous territory for them both. 'I'll be back for the launch, I promise.'

Yeah, but then you'll be gone again. Claudia shrugged as she looked at him. 'Don't bother yourself.'

'I want to.'

'Really, there's no need. We've always known where your priorities lay.'

Luke felt lousy. 'Come on, Claude…I don't deserve that.'

Claudia shrugged. 'Just calling it like I see it.'

The unfairness of her statement stung but he chose to plough on. 'I'll be back for the opening,' he reiterated.

'Fine.'

Luke looked at her. He didn't like this cool and collected Claudia. He couldn't decide if he wanted to kiss her or shake her—anything to get some kind of reaction other than just sitting on the bed looking like his leaving was no big deal.

Saying okay and fine as if it were just another day.

'Hell, Claude.' He shook his head. 'You're hard on a man's ego.'

'Yeah, well, newsflash…I'm not here for your ego. I'm sure they'll appreciate it back in *London* though.'

Luke shoved his hands on his hips, deciding that shaking was looking like a good option. 'Fine,' he snapped. 'Have it your way.'

And he turned on his heel and stormed out of the room, slamming the door behind him.

A well of anger lashed Luke's insides as he strode into his room and began to pace up and down his floor. He knew what he was feeling was irrational. He'd made it clear all along that he was leaving and she was telling him it was fine. Telling him to go.

Making it easy for him.

But he knew all about words like *fine* and how women used them. If she wasn't fine with it, why didn't she just bloody well say so? And would it have killed her to show some kind of disappointment? He hadn't expected her to throw herself at his feet and beg him not to go; he hadn't wanted her to cry or cling.

But they'd made a good team, achieved a lot, dragged the Tropicana into the twenty-first century. Yes, there'd been tensions but they'd laughed and joked a lot too, reaffirmed a friendship that had fallen by the wayside.

Some emotion might have been nice. Instead of sitting all calm and cross-legged like some sexy, half-dressed, milk-moustached freaking…yogi!

His stomach took a tumble as his head filled with that vision and Luke clenched his fists. How was it possible to be so angry and want her so much at the same time? How was it possible to be so close to hating her and yet have a massive hard-on for her?

Goddamn it!

He stormed back into her room, not knocking at all this time. The spoon was halfway to her mouth and her eyes flew to his face. He braced his hands on his hips.

'I can't stand this any longer.'

She didn't say anything, just put the spoon back in the glass and waited. And in two strides he was at the bed, he was whisking the glass away and shoving it onto the bedside table, he was pushing her back against the pillows, reaching for the bottom of her awful shirt and in one quick move he'd grabbed both the edges and ripped.

'Luke,' Claudia gasped as buttons flew everywhere and her buttercup-yellow bra was exposed to his view.

'I've been wanting to do that for three damn months,' he growled.

Claudia knew she should be shocked, she should be scandalised, she should be outraged.

.

She *should* be trying to cover herself.

But the truth was he was eating her up with his eyes, burning up everything he touched with his gaze, and she was so turned on she could barely think straight.

'In about ten seconds I'm going to kiss you and then I'm going to go down on you and make you scream so loudly when you come, the whole hotel will be calling the cops, and if you don't want that then you better tell me to leave now.'

Claudia knew she did not have it in her power to tell him to leave. Yes, she should have more self-respect. He was leaving tomorrow and for him this was nothing more than slaking a thirst that had built and built and built over the months.

But she was pretty damn thirsty too and right now she'd take whatever she could get of him.

She didn't answer him; she simply reached down and un-clipped the front opening of her bra.

Luke watched her breasts fall free and groaned. He didn't need any more encouragement. He fell on her, covering her with his body and kissing her into oblivion. Kisses that pulled at his groin and sank talons into the muscles of his belly. Kisses that called to a primal rhythm somewhere inside him. Kisses that wrapped a silken fist around his heart.

Kisses that tasted of pent-up desire and chocolate milk. 'You taste amazing,' he panted against her mouth, moving to kiss her neck. 'God,' he groaned, 'here too,' as his tongue found another sweet spot.

Claudia slid her hands up under his shirt, filling her palms with warm male flesh as she angled her neck to give him greater access. 'Milo...spilt...' she murmured, too far gone to string a coherent sentence together.

Luke groaned, wanting more of that. Wanting more Milo-flavoured Claudia. He pulled away slightly, reaching for the discarded glass on the side table. Claudia mewed in protest as he levered himself up and straddled her body.

'Shh,' he said as he settled on the tops of her thighs,

scooping up a spoonful of chocolate sludge. 'I want to eat chocolate milk off you.' And before she could protest he lowered the spoon to the hollow at the base of her throat and upended it.

Claudia gasped, her back arching, not because it was cold or even particularly runny, but because her nipples beaded instantly into tight, almost painful points. And he went there next, scooping more Milo sludge from the glass and painting it on her nipples, stopping to suck it off thoroughly, reducing her to a whimpering mess before repainting them again, licking it off again and then trailing the spoon down lower. To her belly button, where he played over and over, dousing the hard little button in thick chocolaty sludge, then licking it off, dousing, then licking, dousing then licking and all the while his fingers taunting the stiff points of her nipples until she was almost crazy with it.

He pasted her in Milo right to the edge of her matching yellow underwear and then he was stripping her out of it and she heard the spoon tink against the glass one last time and then she felt the warm sticky ooze of it join the other slickness between her legs.

Somewhere she heard the dull thud of the glass being discarded and then Luke was settling between her thighs, using his big shoulders to push her legs wider and she opened for him shamelessly, bucking when his tongue touched her.

'Luke,' she gasped.

Luke held her fast as he licked every last morsel of salty, chocolaty goodness from between her legs, circling and thrusting, teasing as he went. She was so close, panting and begging him for release, but this was going to be their last time and he wanted to savour every last drop of her. He wanted to feast here as he'd done that first time with her breasts.

He wanted her to remember this for as long as she lived. *He* wanted to remember it as long as *he* lived.

So he refused to give into her wild urgings, staying

right where he was until even he couldn't wait for her to come a second longer. And pushing her over the edge was so, so easy. A few quick flicks in the right place and she screamed—exactly as he'd predicted—her release, holding his head to her and he didn't stop, not even when she begged him to, he just held onto her hips harder and kept going until every last drop of pleasure had been wrung from her.

But even then he didn't stop.

When he was satisfied she was thoroughly spent he was determined to give her more, revive the fire that he knew still flickered. Crawling back up her body, he reefed down his track pants and underwear, his hardness nudging all her soft heat.

Claudia's eyes flew open and she gasped as all his delicious thickness pushed against her. Even though she was limp and exhausted, her body recognised this need on a primal level. Her back arched and she reached for his buttocks, holding him there.

'Yes,' she said, wanting him inside her with a sudden ferocity. Wanting him to stay in her for ever. Loving the loom of him. Loving the bulge of his biceps, loving the proximity of his chest, loving the closeness of his mouth.

Just plain old loving him.

She linked her arms around his neck. 'God, yes, please.'

And when he thrust inside her in one easy move she cried out, knowing she'd never want another man like this.

That only Luke would ever do.

And when he thrust again and again, groaning deep and slow in perfect time, building her quickly, she fought it off, pushed it away, hanging in there with him, desperate to be there with him at the end.

'Damn it, Claude,' he gasped in her ear, 'let go.'

'No,' she panted. 'Not without you.' If this was to be their last time then they were going out together.

Luke grimaced and on one last thrust and a primal groan that sounded as if it had come from the depths of the earth beneath the Tropicana itself, he came, over and over, calling out her name.

Then and only then did she follow him into the light.

Claudia stirred when Luke rolled off her onto his back a few minutes later. His breathing was still irregular, as was hers. They didn't move or say anything for long moments. Then Luke rolled on his side, slid his arm across her belly and pulled her close.

But Claudia resisted. She couldn't do that. She could make love with him one last time, give her something to exist on in the long lonely nights to follow, but she couldn't snuggle with him afterwards as if there were love between them.

As if he weren't leaving tomorrow.

That *would* break her heart and she just couldn't do it.

Luke frowned. 'Claude?'

She rolled on her side, away from him. 'Just go, Luke.'

He slid his hand onto her shoulder. 'Claudia.'

'I'm okay,' she assured, shrugging his hand away. 'I'm fine. But let's not pretend this is something it's not.'

Luke wanted to protest but ultimately he could see her point. They weren't in a relationship. Staying the night with her would just make it harder in the morning. At least this way, they both knew where they stood.

He rolled to his side of the bed and pushed to his feet, adjusting his clothing. A sudden thought struck him. 'You could be pregnant—we didn't use a condom.' Protection had been the last thing on his mind. He'd just needed to be inside her.

'I've been on the pill since I was nineteen, Luke. I'm not pregnant.'

He shoved a hand through his hair. 'I *have* to go, Claude.'

'I know.'

'I told you it was only temporary, that I'd have to go back eventually.'

'I know.'

Luke looked down at her, her back stubbornly turned away. He hated the distance even though he'd been the one to implement it. He felt a sudden urge to explain. 'My divorce...it was...hard. I can't go there again.'

'I'm not asking you to.'

Luke nodded. He knew that. But a part of him couldn't help wish that she had. 'Will I see you tomorrow?'

'I'll be round,' she murmured.

He stared at her back, torn between leaving and climbing back into bed with her—consequences be damned. But he'd learned too much from bitter experience to know the perils of disregarding consequences. 'Goodnight.'

Whether or not she answered he didn't hear as he walked back to his room and shut the interconnecting door with a soft click.

CHAPTER NINETEEN

'ARE YOU OKAY, dear?' her mother asked as Claudia dashed past the reception desk on her way to the kitchen to check the hors d'oeuvres were on track to be served in half an hour.

'Fine and dandy,' she chirped, before disappearing into Tony's domain.

Lena looked at Gloria. Avery and Jonah looked at each other. They were all poised to join the cocktail party down on the beach. 'Oh, dear. I see what you mean.'

'Yup,' Avery murmured. 'She's all *fine and dandy* again.'

'And she's been like that since Luke left?' Gloria asked.

Jonah, looking resplendent in a tux, grimaced. 'Oh, yes. Two whole weeks of her fine and dandiness.'

Gloria tutted as she shook her head. 'My son is an idiot.'

'Yes,' Lena agreed tersely. 'He is.'

Gloria turned distressed eyes onto Jonah. 'Can you talk some sense into him? He'll listen to you.'

Jonah shrugged. 'Unfortunately, Gloria, some things a man just has to figure out for himself.'

'When was he supposed to arrive?' Lena asked.

'Six hours ago,' Gloria confirmed. 'His flight was delayed out of Singapore. Which is why I told him he should have booked an earlier flight, that he was cutting it fine if anything happened.' Disapproval and anxiety laced her voice. 'I think he should have landed by now though.'

Claudia strode from the kitchen, her red gown fluttering around her ankles, 'Okay, are we all ready?' she asked.

'You guys go ahead. I'll wait for Luke,' Gloria said.

'All right,' Claudia said, smiling brightly, refusing to let his looming presence upset her equilibrium.

She'd held it together for the last two weeks just fine; she wasn't going to let his imminent arrival take the gloss off the night they'd all worked so hard towards. Even if she did feel as if she was about to throw up as the nerves in her stomach knotted ever tighter.

Where was he?

She'd been strung tight as a bow all day as the full gamut of emotions had run riot through her body and she wished he'd just get here already. Get the awkward, stilted greetings out of the way so she could enjoy this night she and Avery had been planning for a month.

Instead of waiting for Prince Charming—*à la Captain Sexypants*—like some lovelorn teenager.

'Let's go have some fun,' she said to the people who meant the most to her in the whole world.

The people who *did* love her.

Avery, who was looking as ethereally gorgeous as ever in a smoky silver frock, smiled and looped her arm through Claudia's. 'Let's party,' she said.

Luke glanced at the dash clock in his rented car. Damn it— he was an hour late. He cursed the state of the roads and the interminable stops for roadworks. He cursed the airline. He cursed the rental company that had mixed up his booking.

It seemed everything had conspired against him getting to the Tropicana Nights on time.

His mother, who was fanatically punctual, would not be impressed. And Claudia? No two ways about it—she'd be really pissed at him.

So what else was new?

His heart beat a little faster at the mere thought of seeing her again, angry or not. He'd thought about her obsessively for two weeks. Reruns of their last night together had played over and over in his head.

He hadn't missed the tension; he hadn't missed the temptation. But he *had* missed *her*.

God, how he'd missed her!

A decade in the UK and she'd barely crossed his mind. Three months back in Crescent Cove with her and he could barely think of anything else.

He felt as nervous as a teenager on his first date.

He didn't know what to expect, what he was going to say, how he would feel. How *she* would feel. He just knew coming back, seeing her again, had been the one bright spot in these last two weeks, getting him through interminably long days at the office, days that he'd once thrived on and had now lost their lustre.

He knew it was just jet lag and readjusting to the crappy London weather and having to wear a suit and tie again instead of boardies and a T-shirt. He'd fallen out of the groove and was having a hard time getting back into it. But he hadn't been able to explain how scoring the firm's biggest account to date—an enormous coup—had left him feeling so...underwhelmed.

How working on Jonah's low-budget ad campaign had been more satisfying and stimulating than the slick multimillion-dollar one that had taken up months of his life.

Coming back to Crescent Cove, with an office that looked out over the mighty Pacific and was less than a minute's walk to a beach of the finest powdery white sand, had somehow tripped a switch in his brain that refused to be reset.

A few months ago the only powder he'd cared about was the type that covered the ski fields of St Moritz. Now, he found himself yearning for the sun and the surf.

Another road worker with a stop sign loomed ahead and he raked a frustrated hand through his hair, bringing it down to rub at his smooth jaw as he decelerated. It made him think of Claudia. Of the conversation—the *naked* conversation— he'd had with her about stubble. He'd shaved on the plane.

He didn't know why—years of conditioning, he supposed—but suddenly even that annoyed him.

Shaving twice a day? What the hell for?

The bored-looking road worker stood aside, flipping the sign around and, ignoring the slow sign, Luke accelerated quickly away.

'It's going great, don't you think?' Avery said as she threw her arm around Claudia, who was watching everything from the sidelines.

Claudia nodded. 'It looks amazing!'

And it did. Avery and her vision had transformed the foreshore, where the avenue of palms met the beach, into a fairyland of lights strung through the trees and the nearby foliage.

A jazz band played on a temporary wooden platform that had been erected on the beach. It was large enough for people to dance and some had already taken advantage. The whole atmosphere was magical, the snazzy couples dancing to smooth saxophone notes against the backdrop of a russet ocean sunset were just the icing on the cake.

A roll of red carpet bordered and lit by flaming tiki torches formed a pathway from the foreshore to the spa where guests came and went exclaiming over the wonders of the posh new facility. Another red-carpeted, tiki-lit pathway led to the nearest luxury tent, drawing more appreciative buzz.

With travel agents and influential tourism representatives here both Claudia and Avery were confident they'd be filling the new luxury accommodation before too much longer.

But it wasn't just the business community who were kicking up their heels. Avery's brilliant idea to combine the black-tie launch with a fundraiser for the cyclone-ravaged area had ensured that plenty of locals were also out in force. Prizes of prestigious spa and accommodation packages had been offered and the locals of Crescent Cove had glammed up and brought their wallets.

And all this serenaded by something that no amount of money could buy. The swish of a calm ocean and the kiss of a gentle breeze. The weather had been the one wild card but even it had bowed to Avery's superior organisational skills. It was a gorgeous, crisp, starry North Queensland winter night. The quarter moon was on the rise, the horizon glowed with orange and pinks and the first stars in the velvety evening dazzled like diamonds.

After the destruction of a few months ago, the weather gods were smiling.

The only thing that was missing was Luke.

'I wouldn't have done half as good a job by myself,' Claudia said, dragging her thoughts back from the one topic that could cast a pall over her entire evening. 'Your eye for detail is awesome.'

Avery hugged her harder and they both just watched the spectacle for a few moments. 'Are you sure you're okay, Claude?' Avery ventured after a while. 'You seem really tense. Are you worried about seeing Luke again?'

'I'm fine,' Claudia hastily assured, not wanting her focus derailed. The party was here and now and Luke...

Luke was late.

'And dandy?'

Claudia glanced at her friend. 'Avery.'

'Claude, I love you, you're my best friend. I *hate* seeing you miserable.'

Claudia frowned—miserable? But she'd been killing herself to be chipper and chatty and chirpy. Just good old Claude. *Business as usual.* She glanced at Avery, looked into eyes that knew her way too well.

And she couldn't deal with it now.

'When does Raoul's studio perform?' she asked, looking back to the beach stage as she, not so deftly, changed the subject.

Avery sighed and checked her watch. 'During the hors d'oeuvres. So...soon.'

'Good,' she said. 'I'm starving.'

Even though she knew food was never going to sit well inside her squalling belly.

Luke followed his mother and the jazzy music towards the beach, straightening the bow tie his mother had hastily thrown together for him. The urge to stop in and see the finished spa and the accommodation was strong but he was already late enough. He pulled up short when he entered the clearing on the foreshore.

'Wow,' he said as myriad fairy lights dazzled his eyes and the party atmosphere instantly embraced him.

'It's spectacular, isn't it?' His mother beamed.

'Amazing,' he agreed.

'Claude and Avery have worked so hard,' she said.

Luke nodded. He'd not been involved in too much of the launch preparations, knowing it was in good hands with Avery. But this...this was utterly breathtaking.

His gaze roamed the classy crowd as his mother chatted about the set-up and the number of local dignitaries that were attending. Luke couldn't give a rat's arse that the state minister for tourism was here—he only cared about one person.

One woman.

A procession of waiters filed past him carrying trays laden with finger food, the aromas of garlic and basil lingering in their wake. They dispersed throughout the guests offering a range of gastronomic delights. Jonah spotted him and strode over to greet him, bringing somebody with him.

'You don't scrub up so bad, old friend.' Luke grinned, shaking Jonah's hand after he'd been introduced to the local tourism council chair.

He shrugged. 'Avery likes me in a tux.'

Luke felt a pang in his chest at the goofy smile Jonah had plastered to his face. As if he already knew how lucky he was going to get later.

The three of them made small talk about the resort and

the long-term recovery of the area as the waiters came around and entertainment took to the stage but Luke was too distracted to eat or be entertained. Too distracted for local politics as he surreptitiously searched the crowd for one particular person. He finally spotted her standing to one side with Avery and, damn, if she wasn't wearing *that* dress.

Everything lurched inside him.

For some reason he'd expected to see her in her usual travesty of polyester—ridiculous really, given that they were both at a black-tie cocktail party. Not that it would have mattered had she been in her uniform. She looked equally good in both, not to mention the fact that he'd helped her out of both in varying degrees of urgency.

She had her hair swept up as it had been that night in Cairns, a frangipani tucked behind her ear.

Do not think about that night in Cairns.

But it was hard not to. There wasn't one part of him that didn't rejoice in seeing her. That didn't want to wrap her up in his arms. That didn't want to drag her away from this party and have his wicked way with her.

Two weeks had felt like two decades and he was gripped by a fierce yearning to be deep inside her again.

Relief flowed through him at his strong physical reaction. He'd been confused by his feelings, unsure of how he felt about somebody he shouldn't be feeling those kinds of things for. Somebody who didn't want to feel them either. But sex he understood. Sex he could pigeonhole. Sex was biology and natural urges.

It wasn't emotional; it was physical.

He'd been lusting after her. And that was an easy fix.

He was just about to stop making polite conversation and excuse himself when a familiar guy in a tuxedo approached Claudia.

Raoul.

A surge of pure possession filled him as Raoul said something to her and both she and Avery laughed.

His heart thudded in his chest as the Spanish charmer flirted easily. Suddenly Luke wasn't feeling so sure of himself.

Suddenly this was a whole new ballgame. Biology, natural urges, lust—they all felt frivolous.

What he was feeling now, watching Raoul with Claudia, was much more primal.

Much deeper. Much more profound.

He watched as Raoul took Claudia's hand and led her to the dance floor and he had to suppress a roar of outrage that rose in his chest.

No!

It was like Cairns all over again. Except a thousand times worse because Claudia was the woman he loved—yes, he *loved* her! —and he wasn't into sharing.

'Excuse me,' he said, interrupting the conversation he hadn't really been listening to anyway. 'I'm sorry,' he apologised. 'There's somebody I really have to see.'

Jonah glanced across to where Luke was looking and nodded. He held out his hand and shook Luke's. 'Go get her, man.'

Unfortunately Luke was waylaid a couple of times but he managed to get to the stage just as the song was ending.

Perfect timing.

'Claude.'

Claudia stilled in the circle of Raoul's arms as a very familiar accent turned her legs to jelly. She leaned in to Raoul for a moment for support and, bless him, he ignored the thunder on Luke's face and let her.

'Mi querida. Are you okay?'

Claudia nodded as she pulled away from him. 'Thanks, Raoul. I'm fine.'

For a moment Claudia thought Raoul was going to challenge Luke, but she gave his arm a squeeze. 'I'll see you later,' she said.

Raoul, ever the gentleman, bowed slightly and took his

leave. Claudia watched him weave through the dancers, collecting herself for a moment before turning to face Luke.

Luke in a tux.

Her stomach dropped at the mere sight of him, her heart rattling along like the lid on a steaming kettle. But she was determined to play it cool.

'You made it,' she said as he held out his arms and she slid into a polite waltz stance and started moving, careful to keep her distance, hoping he couldn't feel the flutter of her pulse at her wrist. 'I thought you must have changed your mind.'

She felt him tense for a moment. 'I said I would be here. I'm here.'

'Why, Luke?'

Claudia was proud of the steadiness of her voice, considering she wanted to stamp her foot and beat her hands against his chest like a spoilt princess or a toddler having a tantrum.

'What's the point when you're just going to turn around and go back to London? It's a long way to come for three lousy days.'

It had been two weeks since Luke had wanted to shake her but only a minute back in her company and the urge returned with a vengeance. 'Because I love you, you irritating woman,' he said, then promptly dipped her and pashed her in front of everyone.

CHAPTER TWENTY

DESPITE HER SHOCK, it didn't take Claudia's heart—or hormones—long to betray her. Her senses filled up with him and she clung to his lapels, kissing him back, two weeks of sexual frustration bubbling up inside her.

It wasn't until the racket of applause finally penetrated their passionate bubble that sense returned and Claudia pushed against his chest, struggling for release. He yanked her up and let her go to more applause from the crowd.

She smiled awkwardly for a moment, then glared at him before muttering, 'Follow me.'

She marched ahead, furious with him and herself. She kicked her stilettos off as she hit the beach, leaving them where they were as she gathered the hem of her dress and made a beeline for the shoreline, conscious of him following more sedately behind.

'How dare you?' she said, turning on him when she was close enough to the water to drown him in it should the urge take over.

Luke held up his hands. 'Claude.'

'Don't you Claude me,' she snapped. 'Don't you come here acting all he-man. All...' she took in his particular brand of delicious in his tuxedo and nearly swooned at his feet '...Captain Sexypants and act like a Neanderthal and expect me to drop at your feet.'

Captain Sexypants? 'Okay.'

'And don't you okay me either,' she seethed, completely oblivious to the romance of the stars overhead and the lapping waves. 'You expect me to believe that you suddenly love me? That this isn't about you being a horny, jealous, possessive jerk?'

Luke had to admit she made a good point. 'Oh, no, it's about all of those things as well,' he admitted candidly. 'When I saw you across the avenue before, it was absolutely about getting you into bed in the fastest possible way. To be honest, it was a relief to feel such a strong physical connection because then I didn't have to think about anything deeper. And then Raoul showed...'

'And you decided you'd come over all territorial and stake your claim?'

Luke wasn't going to apologise for going after what he wanted. A decade in advertising had taught him to hold firm. 'No. I realised what I feel for you goes way beyond the physical.'

Claudia snorted. She refused to let his pretty words sway her. 'Really? Well, too bad. You can't just waltz in here, throw the L word around and use me for three days before you waltz out again. I'm not going to be your little Aussie bonk-buddy.'

'I'm not interested in something casual. I love you, Claudia Davis.'

Claudia shook her head, quashing the excited flutter in her chest. No. She wasn't falling for that. 'You told me two weeks ago that you *couldn't go there again* after your divorce. You expect me to believe that's all changed in just two weeks? That you're suddenly over the most emotionally devastating experience of your life and that you've fallen in love with me? In *two weeks*?'

Luke shook his head. 'Tonight, actually. I fell in love with you tonight.'

'Oh, *great*. That's *so* much better,' Claudia said, folding her arms across her chest.

'What happened with Philippa...the divorce...you're right, it was devastating and I've been clinging to that as an excuse to focus on my career. But I looked across at you tonight and suddenly, all the hurt and humiliation, none of it mattered any more. Yes, I loved Philippa but the truth is, I didn't *fall* in love with her. Not like just now.'

He took a step closer to Claudia because he needed her to hear him. 'We fell into a relationship, we were a convenient couple. We were always at work together, we had a lot in common but I didn't *know* her. Not like I know you. You've been part of the fabric of my life for ever. You're in my DNA, Claude.'

Claudia glared at him, not sure she liked the biological comparison. 'How romantic. I sound like a disease.'

Luke ignored her sarcasm. 'I guess you are,' he admitted. 'You infected me a long time ago and you've been lying dormant inside me until today and now you've totally overrun me. I can't believe it's taken me so long to see what was right in front of me.'

Claudia wanted nothing more than to throw herself into his arms. To take his words at face value and make a grab for her happiness while it was standing right in front of her. But it all just seemed too good to be true. Could love between old friends ever be that simple?

He lived on the other side of the world, for crying out loud!

'Oh, yeah, and how do you see it working between us?' she demanded. 'With you in London and me here?'

Luke shrugged, unfazed. It had taken him a long time to trust enough to love another woman—he wasn't going to do it by halves. 'I don't want to be anywhere you're not and if that means here then so be it.'

Claudia couldn't believe the words coming from his mouth. In just about every way possible it was exactly what she'd wanted to hear. Except *if that means here* was hardly a ringing endorsement. She'd loved Luke most of her life— he'd definitely been in *her* DNA. She knew how much he'd wanted London. How much he'd wanted to be at the forefront of the global advertising industry.

How long before he resented his choice? Before he resented her?

'Come on, Claude,' he murmured. 'I think you might love me too. Give me a chance.'

Claudia looked at him and shook her head, her heart breaking just a little bit more. Of course she loved him. She loved everything about him. Including his pride and his self-respect and how much his career was wrapped up in that.

'So what are you going to do?' she asked. 'Play hotel manager with me? Something you've already rejected?'

'No.' Luke shook his head. He loved the Tropicana but he needed something else. 'Start my own business here, I guess.'

Claudia snorted—it didn't sound as if he'd put a whole lot of thought into it. 'You *guess*?'

Luke raked a frustrated hand through his hair. 'I know it sounds like I'm making this up as I go along but I didn't realise how...over London I was until I came back here. I'd put my dissatisfaction down to work...to the divorce. It wasn't until I came here I realised... This place kind of got to me again. I took it for granted growing up—that was stupid. I really enjoyed working on Jonah's budget campaign. It felt...grass roots. I think I could make that into something.'

Luke surprised even himself with his words but it suddenly felt *right*. Like being here with Claudia did.

'I thought you needed the bright lights?'

'Yeah,' he admitted. 'I did. But I was eighteen, Claude. I've been there and done that. People are allowed to change their minds.'

'I didn't.'

Luke smiled. That was just one of the things he loved about her—ever since his mother had given her that clip-board for Christmas, she'd been so sure.

'People are allowed to stay the same as well.'

Claudia looked at his beautiful face, nicely delineated by the slither of moonlight emanating from the quarter moon.

Thanks to his close shave she could see every line and dip of his jaw and cheeks; she could even make out the remnant of his Crescent Cove tan not yet faded after two weeks in rainy London.

She loved it. Loved every plane and angle. She even loved the ruthless smoothness of his face. But it was a blaring reminder of who he really was. She took a couple of paces towards him, lifted her hand and ran her fingers over his face. He watched her as she caressed his cheek, his jaw, his chin. The top of his lip.

All perfectly smooth. Perfectly London.

Not Crescent Cove.

'You shaved on the plane?'

Luke nodded. 'Of course.'

Claudia dropped her hand. He thought he wanted to be here with her? She didn't think so. Initially maybe when there was lots of sex and sunshine, and then what, when his business didn't match up to his expectations and the bright lights called again? She couldn't risk it. Having him for a while only to lose him again?

Maybe he did love her—her breath caught at the thought, her heart tap-danced in her chest, but she quashed them instantly. She just didn't think he'd thought it through properly. He was acting on lust and desire and a screwed-up sense of possession and she needed more than his jealous bullshit.

'I have to get back,' she said.

Luke took a pace towards her, worried at the sadness, the finality in her tone. 'Claude.'

'Don't,' she said. 'Don't come here with half-arsed, on-the-fly plans.' She picked her hem up again. 'I have to get back,' she said, turning away.

Luke watched her go, frustrated by her stubbornness but encouraged. 'You never told me if you loved me,' he called after her.

She turned to face him, walking slowly backwards. 'I've

always loved you. Doesn't mean it's enough,' she said before turning her back on him again.

Luke knew that was true. But it was a start.

Claudia was in her office working on the housekeeping roster, or pretending to anyway, the next morning when her mother knocked on the door. 'Thought you might like a cuppa,' she said.

Claudia smiled. 'Thanks.' She often thought rosters should be done with a bottle of vodka but a cup of tea would suffice.

'Last night was a huge success,' her mother said as she sat in the chair on the other side of the desk. 'The phone's been running hot down at the retreat all morning.'

'Yes. And we raised fifty grand too. Not bad at all.'

They chatted for a while about the party and the Tropicana before her mother gave her *that* look.

'I saw you and Luke disappear down to the beach last night.'

Claudia almost told her to stop but she'd noticed things were a little tense between her and Gloria and she didn't want that. Maybe if they knew the truth they'd see there was never going to be anything between her and Luke.

'It's never going to happen, Mum. We want different things.'

Her mother put down her cup of tea. 'Claude…we didn't give you this place to tie you down, to act like some kind of anchor to keep you here. If you want to be with Luke and he's on the other side of the world then go and be with him. Do whatever you need to do. We can get managers in. I know you love the Tropicana but it's not worth losing someone you love over.'

Claudia blinked, mentally rejecting the suggestion outright. Leave the Tropicana? It had never occurred to her. She stared at her mother, who looked deadly serious.

'It is okay, you know.'

Claudia opened her mouth to tell her mother no, but her quiet words of acceptance hit like a truck. Was it okay?

Maybe she'd been waiting for permission all these years. For someone to say it *was* okay to leave.

The thought was foreign; she'd never wanted to do anything else, but hadn't Luke said last night that people were allowed to change their minds?

What would she do, who could she be if she stepped outside the security of the Tropicana?

The thought was terrifying but if she had Luke?

She put her cup of tea down, her heart racing a little as she stood. 'Thanks, Mum.'

She smiled back. 'He's down at the beach.'

Luke stood on the near-deserted beach, his ankles in the water, looking at the Tropicana glowing white and proud in the morning sun like the glorious old relic she was. He could see the new spa building through the foliage and a couple of the luxury tents. In a year's time the foliage regrowth would obscure most of it, hopefully.

A surge of satisfaction rose in his chest. He was looking forward to that.

Now he understood what Claudia had been rabbiting on about every time she mentioned their legacy. This place—the place of his childhood, the legacy of his heart—was in his DNA as surely as she was.

Sure, he'd thrived in London. Hell, he'd *needed* London. He'd had to go away to appreciate what he'd really had. What had been right under his nose.

Including Claudia.

But he got it now.

A movement in his peripheral vision caught his eye and he glanced over to find Claudia coming his way looking resplendent in polyester and a ponytail. Avery had shown him the new sample uniform last night and it was a vast improvement but in some ways he'd be sorry to see the old, ugly one go—it had some very hot memories.

She didn't bother greeting him, just stood in front of him with folded arms and said, 'You love me?'

Luke's heart pounded. Could this be...? 'Uh-huh.'

She looked at him a bit longer. 'I'll come to London with you,' she said and turned to go.

Luke frowned. Wait. *What?* 'No.'

Claudia whipped around. 'What do you mean, no? You love me, I love you. Let's just go to London already.'

Luke chuckled at her crankiness. 'No,' he said again.

'I swear to God, Luke, I'm trying to compromise here.'

'No, you're not. You're trying to sacrifice what you want for what you *think* I want.'

'London is where your career is. I'm not going to hold you back.'

'I don't care about London. Not any more. But you... *you* care about that...' he pointed to the Tropicana '...and here's a newsflash—I do too. I can do my job anywhere. I don't need a fancy office or a city skyline. But there's only one Tropicana.'

Claudia glared at him looking all cool and clean-shaven. Even in his boardies and T-shirt the man screamed London. 'You're being impossible.'

He chuckled again. 'I don't think I'm the only one.'

She shook her head and turned on her heel and marched away.

The following morning, after another long, restless night with her on the *other* side of the connecting door, Luke looked at himself in the bathroom mirror.

He knew women found him attractive. He knew Claudia found him *very* attractive. Hell—she loved him. She'd always loved him. That was what she'd told him. So why couldn't he get her to take the leap with him?

He rubbed his hands through his hair in frustration and then across his jaw. The slight rasp of his whiskers had him reaching automatically for his shaving cream and he opened his palm and squirted a dollop in, watching it foam up.

He slapped it on, remembering how Claudia had touched his face the other night and the conversation they'd had in bed when she'd suggested he grew some stubble. Shaving was London, he'd told her, stubble was Crescent Cove.

His hand stopped then as an idea slowly dawned and he smiled at his reflection before turning on the tap and ducking over the sink to wash it all away.

Claudia looked up from the reception desk a couple of hours later as Luke approached. He was in boardies and a T-shirt and no shoes and there was an overnight shadow on his jaw that did funny things to her equilibrium.

'Morning,' he said, acknowledging both her and Isis. 'Jonah and I are heading north to catch some waves,' he said. 'Be back in a couple of hours.'

Claudia couldn't tear her eyes off his jawline. 'Uh-huh,' she said.

She and Isis watched him walk away. 'Mmm. Captain Sexy-Stubble,' Isis murmured.

The next morning was the same. More surfing, more unshaven jaw. By the third morning he had a very definite three-day growth and it was all Claudia could do not to reach out and touch it.

'Not shaving these days?' Claudia said, trying to sound nonchalant.

'Nah, shaving's for city boys.' He grinned and winked at Isis before heading out of the door again.

'Oh, he's playing *dirty* now,' Isis said as they watched him walk away.

Claudia pursed her lips, refusing to say anything.

But *damn,* she'd known he'd look hot with stubble.

* * *

She was waiting for him when he returned in the afternoon, the connecting door wide open.

'I know what you're doing,' she said, entering his room as soon as she heard his door open. His boardies were damp and his hair was wet and the shaggy jawline was the cherry on top of his very delicious beach-bum look.

Luke suppressed a smile. 'Oh? What's that?'

She crossed her arms. 'The stubble.'

He stroked the back of his hand up his throat. 'You want to touch it, don't you?' He grinned.

Claudia glared. 'Luke.'

Luke sighed at the reprimand in her voice. 'Claude,' he said, moving towards her until he was just a hand's reach away. 'I've thrown my shaving foam in the bin. I'm not going back to London. I'm *done* with London.'

He reached for her then, tentatively at first, sliding a hand onto her waist. When she didn't push him away, he tugged her closer. He looked into her eyes, a kaleidoscope of conflict.

'*I love you.* I'm setting up business right here and I'm never shaving regularly again. Now how about you stop being all sacrificial and stoic and just kiss me already?'

Claudia wanted to. She wanted to very badly. She wanted to throw caution to the wind and let him ravage her with his stubbly kisses. 'The Tropicana has never been your dream. I can't...' She paused, searching for the right words. 'I wouldn't survive if you decided it wasn't enough for you some time down the track.'

Luke smiled at her gently. 'The Tropicana is big enough for both our dreams. And besides...the Tropicana *is* you and *you're* my dream. *I love you.* Nothing else matters. Nothing.'

He leaned into her neck and nuzzled it where her pulse beat frantically and was satisfied by her low, throaty moan.

'Tell me you love me,' he said, pulling away.

Claudia ran a finger along his jawline from ear to chin, loving the spikiness against her skin. 'You know I do.'

Luke went for her throat again, moving higher this time. 'Tell me.'

Claudia angled her neck and shut her eyes as a wave of goose bumps sounded a warning call to the rest of her body. 'I love you.'

And, *damn*, didn't it feel good to get it off her chest?

Luke nipped her triumphantly and she gasped, grabbing two handfuls of his shirt and pulling him closer. 'Don't stop,' she moaned. She'd been lying awake for nights thinking about him in the next room, grinding her heels into the bed to stop herself from going to him.

Luke smiled as he stroked his tongue where his teeth had just been. 'I'm never going to stop,' he said.

'I'm going to hold you to that,' she murmured.

Luke grinned against her neck, then, in one swift movement, picked her up and carried her over to the bed, dumping her in the middle.

His gaze roved over her looking all tousled and sexy despite the uniform. 'Unless you want me to rip that—' he pointed to the hideous polyester '—off you again, I suggest you take it off right now.'

Claudia grinned, grabbed the two edges of her shirt and ripped, buttons flying everywhere.

The new uniforms were arriving tomorrow.

'We are going to be *so* good together.' He grinned.

Claudia smiled up at him, her heart almost too big for her chest. 'Yes, we are.'

EPILOGUE

Six months later

THE STAGE WAS set for a far north Queensland double wedding in the way only Avery could orchestrate. The powdery sand was blindingly white, the ocean was as clear and flat as cut glass, the sky was a stunning blue dome that not one cloud was game enough to besmirch.

Mother Nature knew better than to ruin an Avery Shaw creation.

'It's perfect, Avery,' Claudia whispered, squeezing her best friend's hand as they stood with their fathers before the petal-strewn sandy aisle, waiting for the music to strike up.

'*They're* perfect,' Avery whispered back, looking at their men waiting at the other end.

Claudia nodded. 'Yes, they are,' she agreed as the first violin note rent the tropical air and the guests all turned in their beribboned chairs, then stood, smiling at the brides.

The two women couldn't have looked more different. Avery, dressed in designer squillions, looked all lean and long in her filmy white mermaid gown that brushed the sand, her shoulders bare, her hair falling in long, elegant, surfy waves down her back, a Swarovski crystal flower catching up one side of her locks in dramatic fashion.

Claudia, despite threatening to wear her uniform, looked stunning in a white, georgette slip dress with shoestring straps. It hugged her body close and fluttered around her ankles. She wore her hair swept up as she had that night she and Luke had first made love, a hibiscus flower tucked behind her ear.

The only things in common were their simple frangipani posies.

Luke held out his hand for her and smiled as she reached him and Claudia's heart felt as if it were bursting from her chest. He was looking his shaggy best, all suntanned and stubbly, his hair longer now and sunstreaked.

'You look beautiful,' he murmured.

'So do you.'

And he did, his mocha-coloured trousers and cream shirt showing off his tan and his muscles to perfection. He'd thrived on the challenge of setting up his own business and become honed and fit from his early morning beach runs.

'Are we ready?' the celebrant asked.

Claudia looked at Avery. Her father was murmuring something to her and Claudia was pleased that Avery's parents had set aside their differences and had both travelled from the US to be here for her today. Mr Shaw kissed his daughter on the cheek, then passed her hand to a scrummy-looking Jonah, clad in sand-coloured linen trousers and white linen shirt.

'We're ready,' Jonah said.

Hull, who was sitting beside him, a big white bow attached to his collar, barked in agreement much to everyone's amusement.

And with the mighty Pacific in front of them and their beloved Tropicana behind, the couples pledged their love and fidelity.

'You may kiss your brides,' the celebrant murmured, after the rings were exchanged and the ceremony came to an end.

Jonah whooped and dramatically dipped Avery to much applause. Claudia laughed and shook her head, enjoying their moment until Luke picked her up, her feet dangling well clear of the sand, and twirled her in his arms.

'You've made me happier than I ever knew I could be,' he said.

Claudia smiled, wrapping her arms around his neck. 'I love you,' she said, pulling him close, kissing him with greedy intent.

When they finally surfaced some time later her head was spinning and she grinned at him. 'I feel giddy.'

'Good.' Luke chuckled. 'Because you make *me* giddy.'

And then he twirled her around and around and around beneath the tropical sun.

* * * * *